Sherwin A Goodman

Rick Drago 2
The Missing Prototype

Rick Drago 2
The Missing Prototype

ISBN: 9781777103446

Chapter One

Rick Drago sits at a table in the crowded Tavern at the corner of Cote des Neiges and Barclay Street. He's waiting for a man whom he has never met. Rick frequently glanced at his watch, 19:00 hours was the arranged time of the meeting.

He ordered a Jack Daniels neat. At 19:00 hours, a man got up from a table across the room and joined Rick.

The man introduced himself as David Mercier. The retired head of a significant security firm. The Tavern was busy with customers, most of the workers on their way home from their jobs.

The weather had started to get a little chilly. From his jacket pocket, David took an envelope and slid it across the table to Rick.

"These are pictures of Pierre Cote when he worked with me. I was able to get them out of his file before I retired," David said.

Rick took the photos and looked at them. One of the pictures was a mugshot of a man with curly black hair and a mustache; the other showed a man fully dressed in a uniform. The uniform was a tight fit and showed the man's muscular body. Rick scrutinized the pictures.

"You can keep those," David said, as he took a sip of his beer.

"No, I've seen enough. You can tell me about this fellow Cote," Rick said.

"He was my second-in-command. So when he came up with the idea of sending the prototype out with the armored truck, I thought it was brilliant," said Mercier, as he lit a cigarette.

"No one thought it was unusual for the armed guards to take two sacks when they left the building. From the office window upstairs, we watched as the truck went through the gate without any problem," David continued. "I should have suspected something when the guard at the gate didn't leave the booth. Those guys were taught to inspect any vehicle leaving the building."

"What happened after the armored vehicle went through the gate?"

"I left the office and went home for lunch," Mercier said.

"What time did you find out about the heist?" Rick asked.

"The call came through on my car phone as I was heading back to the office. I drove to the scene. What a horrible sight, the guards shot in the back of their heads." Mercier had no expression on his face as he looked over Rick's left shoulder.

"What did you do after seeing the guards' bodies?"

Mercier shrugged his shoulders."What did I do? I have seen men die before, but nothing like this.

"One guy had a large hole at the back of his head. The police were taking statements from eye-witnesses. I left and went to the office."

"What about Pierre Cote? Did he go to the scene of the heist?" Rick asked.

"Not when I was there; He came after I returned to the office. He vanished that same weekend, so did the prototype. Pierre was last seen boarding a flight to Toronto, but that was a few years ago."

Rick looked at his watch. The time was now twenty-one hours. It had been two hours since David had joined him to tell his story.

The Tavern was now full, some of the people spoke English, some spoke French, they all drank and ate with loud laughter.

"Mr. Drago, I saw Pierre Cote last week on my way back from London, he sat two seats ahead of me. His hair color has changed, his face had a few changes, but I knew it was him."

"Did you speak to him?" Rick asked.

"After we were airborne, I stayed back watching him. There are certain things you learn about people when you've worked with them. And as I watched the man sitting in front of me, I became more convinced that he was Pierre Cote."

"Did you approached him?" Rick asked.

"I waited until the seat belt sign was turned off. I then said. "Pierre, how are you?"

"Sir, you must be mistaken," he said.

"Pierre, don't you remember me? I am David Mercier; We worked together a long time ago. He didn't reply, so I went back to my seat."

"What about the prototype? Did it ever show up?" Rick asked.

"As far as I know, it never did," replied Mercier.

Drago finished his drink. He had met with David at the request of an old friend. David had reached out for help after seeing Pierre on the flight back from London.

"How long were you in Europe?" Rick queried.

"I was there for three weeks. I visited France,

Germany, Switzerland, and England before returning home," David said as he slammed his fist down on the table and spilling his beer. "He got away with it, he pulled it off."

Drago looked at David as he wiped the beer from the table.

"Do you think Pierre is responsible for the theft of the prototype?" Rick Drago asked.

"Yes, he knew that the company wouldn't report the theft of the prototype because it would be bad for business, and he was right."

"Didn't the company do anything to recover the prototype?"

"Yes, they did. The company hired two private detectives. The first one was never seen or heard from again," David said.

"And the second? What did he find?" Rick asked.

"That my friend, we'll never know. He was found sitting at the wheel of his car with his head blown off."

"So, what do you want from me?" Rick asked

"After I retired from the company, I was approached by the people who invested their money in the prototype. They would like to have it recovered. The company I used to work for, was contracted to build a section of the prototype,"David said while he reached into the inside pocket of his coat, produced a brown envelope, and slid it across the table to Drago.

"I hope this will cover the cost of your expenses coming here."

Rick slid it back. "I am sorry," he said." But that won't be necessary. I came here at the request of an old friend. He told me that you might be able to shed some light on what happened to a friend of mine in the Island of Haiti."

"That's it, Mr. Drago. Your friend was the brother-in-law of Pierre Cote. Frank Allen's sister is married to Pierre. We don't have all the facts about Frank's death, but I know the other section of the prototype is complete. I thought that maybe Frank was doing some investigation , found out a few things, and got killed," Mercier said.

Rick had heard enough. It all made sense now.

"Goodbye, David," he said as they shook hands.

Rick knew very well what he had to do, and this one was personal. He and Frank had been friends since the war.

Although they didn't see each other often, they had remained friends. Rick had urged Frank to take the job in Haiti Now, he was dead.

The streets were brightly lit the skies clear,

and full of stars. Rick had parked his car a block away from the Tavern.

He flipped the collars of his coat and started walking, something in the shadow of a building caught his attention. He moved swiftly with both hands in his coat pocket.

From the shadow of the building, a man walked towards him. Suddenly there was a flash as the man drew a knife and attacked, eyes wide with a look of excitement.

The guy took a swipe with the knife as Rick ducked under the swinging hand at the same time sweeping with his right foot, knocking the man to the ground. Both of them rolled with Rick holding onto the hand that held the knife.

They came to a stop against a building. Rick on top of the man and wrenched the knife out of his hand. He then held the blade to the man's throat. Immediately Rick recognized him for one of two men who had been sitting at a corner table in the Tavern.

"Easy!" Rick advised. "Just take it easy!" There was a look of madness on the man's face while he struggled to get free from the vise-like grip Rick had on his hands.

"Who hired you?" Still no answer.

The man kept moving his head from side to side. His actions caused the knife to mark his throat. The man then brought his upper body up using all of his strength, creating the blade to pierce deeply into his throat. It became apparent to Rick that this guy would rather die than answer his questions.

Where was his partner? Rick thought to himself while he stood with his back against the building and listened, hearing nothing, he moved swiftly to his car, got in, and drove to the hotel. He thought about David and hoped he had made it home safely.

Rick entered his suite on the 12th floor of the hotel. Without turning the light on, he walked to the window, and looked out over the city. Cars were parked on both sides of the street.

A red light in one of them caught his attention. He left the window and walked towards the bed as he started to undress.

"Stay where you are!" The voice came from the clothes closet.

He followed the sound of the voice and saw the nozzle of a gun pointed at him.

The man in the closet said. "Who are you? And what do you want with David Mercier?"

"To answer the first question," Rick said. "You obviously know who I am, you're in my suite, and to the second question. What business is it of yours?"

"Don't get smart with me!"

"Or what? You'll shoot me?" "I don't think so. If not, you would have done it when I entered the suite."

"I am here to warn you. Leave this alone!" the man said as he went and slammed his way out of the door.

Rick waited a few minutes before switching the lights on. The drawers were pulled out, the bed unmade.

He left the suite and headed downstairs. Reaching the lobby, he looked around, but the man was not there. Rick made his way out the door and into the cold night air.

He walked briskly in the direction he had seen the red light in the parked car. Many of the vehicles were not there, including the one with the smoker.

Rick went back to the hotel and called David from the payphone in the lobby. "Hello," David said.

"Rick Drago here. They're some developments since I last saw you. Have you discussed this matter with anyone else?"

"Of course not," David said.

"I think Pierre has sent someone to keep an eye on you. Your life could be in danger," Drago said.

"I'm an old man. Why would Pierre want to

keep an eye on me?" Mercier asked.

"He probably thinks you know too much and can hurt him. I've got to go now. I'll telephone you in a couple of days, and remember, don't talk to anyone!" Rick commanded.

Rick hung up the phone before David could say anything and went back to his suite. The next morning, he paid his bill and checked out, two hours later he was at the airport boarding a flight to Toronto. Rick settled in his seat, he thought about what had happened since he met with David Mercier. Someone wanted him dead. Others sent him a warning.

David was the man in charge of security at the time of the theft. Pierre was his second in command. His thoughts were interrupted when the steward asked.

"Sir, can I get you something to drink?"

"Yes, Jack Daniels, if you have it," replied Rick. After receiving his drink, he tilted his chair back and sipped the whiskey, turned his head, and watched the clouds go by his window.

Sitting next to him was a nicely tanned woman, expensively dressed. Rick stared at her beautiful breast that seemed to move with every breath she took. She turned her head, looked at him, smiled, and closed her eyes.

Rick finished his whiskey and closed his eyes. He trained himself to be a light sleeper. Rick heard a voice saying.

"Sir. Sir," the steward said.

Rick opened his eyes. The steward was looking at him.

"We'll be landing in an hour. Would you care to have something else?"

"Yes, I'll like another whiskey," Rick replied.

The plane taxied to a stop. He waited until the passengers had left the plane, he watched the faces as they passed by his seat. No one looked familiar to him.

He reached the luggage ramp just in time to see the woman who had sat next to him walking away, followed by a man dressed in a chauffeur uniform carrying her luggage.

Rick got his luggage and headed out to the limousine section. The man that carried the lady's bags approached him.

"Sir. Madam would like to offer you a ride to your hotel." Rick followed the chauffeur and got into the back seat.

"I'm glad you've accepted my offer, Mr...." she said.

"Rick Drago," he replied. "My friends call me, Rick."

"Can I call you Rick? I'd like to be one of your friends."

She rested her hand on Rick's and said."My name is Charlotte Kingsley."

"Pleased to meet you."

"Where are you staying, Rick?"

"I have a reservation at the Sheraton Hotel downtown Toronto."

"I don't live far from there. Would you like to come with me or check into the hotel first?"

"I'll go with you." he replied.

The house was more like a mansion; Drago followed her, beginning to wonder if she was married or single.

Many paintings hung on the walls. The driver brought in her luggage, she dismissed the chauffeur after informing him not to take Rick's bags from the car, and that he'll be taking Mr. Drago to the hotel when he's ready to leave.

"Help yourself if you care to have something to drink. I'll get into something more comfortable. If you want to freshen up, use the other bathroom. You'll find what you need in there," Charlotte said.

She turned and walked away. Drago liked the way she walked away swinging her hips, the dress on her revealing all the curves of her body.

Rick looked around the room. One portrait of a senior man was the only picture of anyone hanging on the wall with the other paintings. He was admiring the view when she returned from the bathroom.

"That's my dad," she said. "More correctly, my father-in-law. He died a few years ago."

"I'm sorry," Rick sympathies.

"Nothing to be sorry about. He had a great life, "Charlotte said.

"Can I make you something?" Rick Drago asked.

"Yes, I'll have a martini, double Vermouth, single Gin," she replied.

Rick made her the drink and handed it to her.

"You're still fully dressed," she said. "Are you going to freshen up?"

"I didn't want to search for the other bathroom; I decided to wait and let you show it to me."

"Follow me!" she said, taking Rick by the hand and leading him to the other bedroom, which also had its bathroom.

Charlotte wore nothing under her robe. She sat on the edge of the bed and watched as Drago got undressed, taking a sip of her martini and running her tongue over her lips.

Rick stare at her exposed breasts; he wanted to reach out and touch one but he decided instead to take a bath. He turned and went into the bathroom.

The sight of his muscular body made Charlotte's heart start to beat more rapidly..

The thought of making love to Rick had her

juices flowing. She couldn't remember ever looking at a man who made her feel like this, wanting and hungry.

The feeling had become unbearable, Charlotte loosen the waistband of her robe and let it fall to the rug as she got up.

She entered the bathroom as Rick was drying his body. Charlotte dropped to her knees and took his dick in her mouth. Rick's manhood began to swell as her tongue moved up and down.

She began to moan, lick, suck, and sometimes give a teasing nibble as his cock grew bigger. He picked her up and set her ass on the dresser table, spread her legs, and entered her. The sound of joy escaped from her mouth.

He then lifted her from the table and walked the couple of steps to the bed.

"You feel so good. I don't want you to stop," Charlotte whispered in his ear.

Rick pushed his cock deep into her, bringing her to a climax with the feeling of ecstasy she couldn't remember ever having before. Charlotte contracted her vagina with every squirt as he come in her.

Rick's hands were exploring her body. His lips kissed her all over, bringing her to another orgasm.

Weak, exhausted, and satisfied, she lay with

her legs spread apart and a smile on her face. Charlotte fell asleep, and when she opened her eyes, Rick was getting dressed.

"Are you still going to the hotel? I was hoping you would stay here." Charlotte queried.

"I have some important business to take care of. Then, I'll see you later," Rick replied.

"Okay, my driver will take you to the hotel."

"I must go now," Rick said.

Charlotte waved jauntily at Rick as the Mercedes pulled out of the driveway and sped away.

The traffic on the highway moved steadily. Rick thought about Charlotte and many other women he had come in contact with during his work. The voice of the chauffeur broke his thoughts.

"Your hotel, Sir."

Rick thanked him and checked in.

Shortly after entering his suite, the phone rang, he picked up the receiver.

"Hello," he said.

"This is Diana. I'm calling to confirm the time of the meeting."

"I'll be there," Rick promised.

"How will you get there? Do you have a car?" Diana asked.

"No, I don't have a car."

"I can pick you up if that's alright with you," Diana said.

"Okay, that's alright with me," Rick replied . "What time will you be here?"

"Elevenish."

"Thank you. I'll be ready."

Rick changed his clothes and went downstairs to the dining room, feeling famished after the session with Charlotte. He ordered a steak with a baked potato.

After dinner, Rick returned to his suite and made a call to Dan.

"How's the weather up there in Toronto?" Dan asked.

"A little chilly, not bad for this time of the year," Rick asked.

"How did the meeting go with David?"

"I got the information from him."

"Have you made contact with anyone in Toronto?"

"Yes, a woman named Diana called about the meeting. She promised to pick me up."

"Diana? The General didn't mention anyone named Diana. What is her last name?"

"She didn't mention the last name, and I didn't ask."

"Okay, keep me up to date."

Rick Drago started to hang up the phone, but

before he could turn away, it rang again.

"Hello," Rick said.

"Sir, this is the front desk; someone is on the way up to see you."

"Thank you," Rick replied.

He removed the gun from the hiding place in his bag and held it behind his back. He waited for the knock on the door, he wasn't expecting any visitors and Dan hadn't mentioned anything to him when he spoke to him a few minutes ago. The knock came.

"Yes," said Drago. "Who is it?"

"The General, Rick."

"Just a moment," said Rick as he unlocked the door and stepped a few paces back.

"Come in," Rick commanded

The door opened, and a young man stepped in, followed by an older gentleman, then another man.

"Rick Drago. I'm General Tom Applewaite; these are my two associates Paul and Bob."

"I didn't expect to see you until tomorrow at your place," Rick said.

"I decided to come and see you today; I have to travel to New York in the morning," replied General Applewaite.

"Drink?" Rick asked.

"Yes, replied the General.

Drago poured two Jack Daniels.

"Please sit, General!"Rick exclaimed.

"How did the meeting go with David?" asked General Applewaite.

"It went well, but first, I must ask. How did you come to know David?" Rick asked.

"We met through a mutual friend a long time ago, and we stayed in touch with each other. Why do you ask?" the General queried.

"An attempt was made to stop me shortly after I met him," he continued . "What about his family?"

"He's married and has two daughters. The wife's name is Dorothy, and the girls are Diana and Charlotte," replied The General settling back in his chair.

Tall with black hair with a touch of gray on both sides, he looked muscular and in shape.

"You looked puzzled, Rick," the General said.

"I think one of his daughters was on the flight from Montreal, the one named Charlotte, but the last name is Kingsley," Rick said.

"Yes, that's Charlotte, Kingsley is her married name." the General replied.

"I was at her home and saw a picture of an old man she told me it was her father," Rick said.

"After her divorce from his son, they stayed very close. That's her father-in-law," said General Applewaite.

"And Diana? Who phoned me about the

meeting?" Rick queried.

"Yes, that's the sister she works for me," replied the General.

Rick got up and poured himself another drink. "Do you care to have another drink?" Rick asked.

"Yes, I'll have another, thank you," replied the General. "We ran a check on Pierre Cote a few weeks ago. It looks as if he's gone into hiding."

"Someone doesn't want anyone finding Pierre Cote," he said. "Someone attacked me after my meeting with David, and then I had a visitor in my suite in Montreal.

The man on the street had tickets for a flight to London, England leaving Montreal at 4 pm tomorrow," Rick said.

"We found out the attacker on the street works as an enforcer for a crime family and is known to the crime squad."

"The guy in my suite left no prints. I checked with my gadget the man was very professional."

"Here is your ticket, you're on that flight to England," said the General. "This is why I came today instead of waiting for tomorrow, plus having to travel to New York."

Chapter Two

The next day found Rick Drago en route to London. He had plenty to think about during the long flight.

Rick had learned about David Mercier's two daughters, Charlotte and Diana. The General showed him a picture of his contact in London who would meet him at the airport.

One of the men at the tavern where Rick met with David Mercier was on the flight to London. He was in the company of another man sitting a couple seats behind Drago.

Rick didn't know if the guy recognized him. After clearing security.

Drago was met at the airport by Michael Strong, a tall, muscular, broad shoulder black man.

Michael Strong was an ex MI6, who got injured on the job and was assigned to desk duty as a field agent. He found it hard to adjust and decided to open a security firm, but still worked the books for the company.

"Please to meet you, Mr. Drago," said Michael with his hand extended.

The two men shook hands as Rick began looking around.

"What's wrong?" Michael asked.

"I'm looking for someone," Rick Drago replied.

"A friend of yours?" Michael asked.

"No, someone of interest. I saw him in Montreal a few days ago and on the plane," Rick said.

"You didn't see him at the luggage ramp?" Michael asked.

"No," Rick Drago replied.

"What is he wearing?" Michael asked.

"He's tall, sandy hair and wearing a plaid jacket," said Drago. "Did you see anyone fitting the description?"

"No, I didn't," Michael replied.

The ride to the hotel took thirty minutes, Drago checked in, then he and Michael enter the dining room. After they were seated Rick went back to the front desk and asked that any calls for him should be sent to the dining area.

Then he returned and joined Michael.

"He followed us," Rick shrugged.

"Who followed us?" Michael asked.

"The man who was on the flight is here," Rick explained.

Michael turned his head and saw two men standing at the front desk, talking to the clerk. Michael got up from the table and went out to the car, moments later, the men came out and got into a Silver- Grey Rover and left.

Drago came out, got into the car with Michael, and followed the Rover as it headed for the docks.

"Do you think he's leaving on a ship?" Michael asked.

"Could be meeting someone," Drago replied.

The Rover stopped, two men got out and went on board the ship.

"How do you want to play this?" Michael asked.

"Let's wait a couple of minutes," Rick replied.

The skies were grey with dark clouds, and there was mist over the water in the harbor. After five minutes, Drago said. "Let's go."

Michael move the Jaguar along the waterfront, reaching the ship, they realized it was a floating restaurant. The sign read D.I.M.E restaurant, open daily from eleven o'clock in the morning until three o'clock the following morning. Strong wrote down the number of the license plate on the Rover.

"I'll have this plate checked for ownership," Michael said.

"Run a check on the restaurant and find out all you can about the people who own it," Rick suggested.

A tall red-haired woman came from the Restaurant and got into a sports car, made a U-turn, and headed in the direction of Michael and Drago.

"Should we follow her?" Michael asked.

"No. We'll come back later," Rick said.

With her hair blowing in the wind, the woman sped by in the Mercedes sports car.

"I'll go back to the hotel and get some much-needed rest," Rick sighed.

"I'll check on you later today," Michael promised stopping the car at the front of the hotel.

Rick got out of the car, then entered the hotel and got in the elevator, he saw the tall figure of the woman from the ship when he got off the lift.

"What kept you?" she asked." I was about to leave."

"Who are you?" Rick asked.

"I'm Jenny Davies. I have a message for you, that is if you're Rick Drago."

"Who sent the message?" Rick asked.

"It's from David Mercier," replied the woman.

Rick unlocked the door to his suite and stepped in.

"Aren't you going to invite me in?" Jenny asked smiling.

"Yes, please come in," Rick said, as he held the door open for Jenny to enter. Her eyes filled with excitement, and the low-cut dress she was wearing revealed the top of her breasts.

"What is the message?" Rick asked gesturing for her to sit at the table.

"Are you Canadians, all business and no play?" she asked after she sat down..

"First of all, I'm not a Canadian, and second, I like to play,"Rick replied sitting next to Jenny..

"Good," Jenny said.

She removed the gloves from her hand and placed them on the table with her purse, then tried to kiss Rick on his cheek.

"If you don't mind, I'll like to hear what you came here to tell me," Rick insisted.

Jenny got up from the table, so did Rick. She held his hand and led him to the bed, Jenny gave him a push, Rick fell back onto the bed.

"I heard so much about you, feels like I've known you for a long time," Jenny said.

She tried to kiss him on the lips. Drago rolled her over. With a smile on her face, she turned him back on his back, this time removing a pin from her hair. She tried to stick Rick in his neck.

With both feet, Rick pushed, sending her backward. Jenny lost her balance and hit the back of her head against the table.

A small trace of blood appeared at the corner of her mouth. Rick rushed off the bed and checked her pulse. She was dead.

He made a call to Michael and explained what had happened; Michael made arrangements to have the cleaner come and take care of the problem.

In Jenny's purse, Rick found a card with an invite to meet Wong. Rick and Michael left the suite and went to Michael's office. They waited for a call from the cleaner about the mess at the Hotel.

Michael showed Drago around the office. After the tour, the two men went back to Rick's suite at the Hotel. Everything was in place as if nothing had happened.

Drago changed his clothes and they headed for the D.I.M.E Restaurant to meet with Lo Wong. The waitress seated them at a table and asked what they would like to drink.

"I'll have a Jack Daniels with ice," said Rick Drago

"And you, Sir, what will you have?" asked the waitress, looking at Michael.

"I'll have a single malt, no ice," Michael replied.

The woman nodded before bringing out a few drinks with a menu.

"I'm here to see Lo Wong. Is he here?" Drago took a sip of the whiskey handing her the card.

"Yes, he's here," said the woman as she turned to walks away.

A few minutes later, two large men approached the table.

"Mr. Wong will see you now," declared the bigger of the two. Rick and Michael stood up giving each other knowing looks.

"Only you," one of them pointing at Drago. Michael sat back down as his companion went to see Wong, while one of the men stayed close to their table.

Drago followed the man up the stairs, along a wide corridor until they reached a room at the end. Upon entering, Rick was searched, and the smell of opium greeted his nose. Inside a small man sat behind a desk with a pipe in his mouth.

"Mr. Rick Drago, please take a seat," said the man sitting behind the desk, more like ordered, gesturing to the chairs in front of him.

"You're Wong?" Drago asked as he sat.

"Yes, and I think we should talk," Wong removed the pipe from his mouth with a grim smile.

"Talk about what?" Rick asked with a hint of sarcasm in his voice.

"You are a worthy adversary. An interesting and slippery man indeed," Wong replied, voice unwaveringly calm.

"Wong," Rick said before being cut off.

"Lo. My friends call me Lo. Do you want to be my friend? Being my friend has many advantages," Lo Wong interrupted, eyeing him curiously.

Rick thought Lo Wong looked ridiculous sitting in such a large chair, he was a small man wearing thick glasses, one who had to have weighed about one hundred and thirty pounds. At a signal from Wong, a tray of drinks was placed onto the table with two drinking glasses.

"Care to join me?" Wong asked. When he didn't answer, Lo poured himself a drink and continued.

"My man in Montreal talked with you and hadn't been heard from since. Now, Jenny went to see you, and I haven't heard from her either. You're a man of great talents, and I could use someone like you on my side of these playing teams," Wong said.

"What game are we playing?" Rick snapped, looking around the room.

One man stood behind Wong, as well as one on each side of the table and two standing at the door.

"Mr. Rick Drago, you met with a man named David Mercier in *Montreal*. I would like to know what he said at that meeting. Let me warned you that I'm not a compassionate man."

"My meeting with David had nothing to do with you," Rick said simply, offering a smirk.

"Let me be the judge of that. I want to know what that old fool told you?"Lo sat back in his chair, waiting.

Drago shrugged."David Mercier wanted me to find a man named Pierre Cote," he finally admitted.

"Pierre Cote! Who is Pierre Cote?" Wong asked.

"I was hoping you could help me find out who and where he is. That's actually why I'm here. There's no other reason for my visit unless you want to give me one."

Rick now crossed his arms and thought. *This son of a bitch is in for a big surprise. If he thinks what happened to the guy in Montreal or to the red-head he sent over to his suite was bad, it will be worse for him.*

"I owe you an apology. Mr. Drago, I could still use a man with your talents working for me."

"I already have a job," Rick said.

Lo Wong stood up for the first time and walked from behind the desk. Rick got up.

"How long will you be staying?" asked Wong.

"Don't know," Rick replied.

"You're welcome here anytime, and if I can be of any assistance, don't hesitate to ask," Wong said as he led Rick to the door.

Rick and Michael then left the Restaurant.

"How did it go?" Michael asked getting behind

the wheel of the car.

"I didn't learn anything about Pierre Cote from Wong, but he was very interested in my meeting with David Mercier."

"Wong knows David Mercier, but doesn't know Pierre Cote?" Michael raised a brow.

"That's right, and David never mentioned anything about Lo Wong when I met with him in Montreal," Rick shrugged.

"Do you believe, Wong?" Michael queried.

"We'll take a look at his office at the Restaurant!"

"The Restaurant closes for only a few hours. They use that time to clean up and prepare the menu for the next day," Michael said. "We'll return after closing time then."

Michael and Rick returned and entered the water; both men wore black wet-suits. They boarded the Restaurant climbing onto the large tires hanging on the side.

Rick was the first to get on board the Floating Restaurant. With Michael close behind, the two men moved into a crouched position. The only light in the dark was at the entrance.

They decided to split up; Both men stopped at the sound of footsteps and voices, with flame from a match while one of them lit a cigarette, Rick saw the faces of the man on the flight and the big man who escorted him to Wong earlier.

Michael attached the silencer to his gun while he got his gadgets ready. They moved towards the two men as quiet as possible, lest they be caught. Michael struck first in almost a blur, the wire from his watch stem now around the neck of the big man while he pull him backward.

Meanwhile, the poor bastard struggled to escape,wheezing at the pressure at his neck. Rick then cut the other guy's throat and neatly caught his body before it hit the floor, making sure to lower it slowly so as not to catch any unwanted attention.

With a nod to one another, they both leaned their ears close to the door to listen.

Both men crept along a corridor heading for the office Rick had visited earlier, before standing outside the door and listening. Hearing nothing they entered to find a dim light burning over the desk. Suddenly there was noise of a toilet flushing.

Rick cursed himself for not questioning one of the men before killing them to find out if anyone else was in the Restaurant.

"I'll take him out," He whispered to Michael as he left the office heading in the direction of the bathroom. This unsuspecting man was just the Janitor doing his nightly cleaning of the Restaurant. Rick quickly locked him in the storeroom after knocking him out.

Michael was already going through drawers in the desk and cabinet. While Rick searched and found a safe behind a painting of the ocean.

"Allow me," Michael gave a mock bow, beginning to pick the safe open. Inside they found money and airline tickets with the names Jenny Daniels and Lo Wong. A sudden noise outside the door caught their attention, and Rick turned off the light on the desk.

The door opened, but no one entered, Rick and Michael stayed hidden.

"Who's there? Come on out!" said a man with a Chinese accent.

Rick moved closer to the door and waited. The figure appeared in the door as Rick made his move, ramming the blade into the belly of the intruder and twisting it. With a grunt, the man fell to the ground with his gut ripped open.

The cigarette he was smoking fell into the wastebasket next to the duo, igniting the paper. Quickly the office filled with smoke.

Rick and Michael not wanting to go around to the front; jumped into the water from where they were and began to swim.

Although they had inhaled a lot of smoke, both men made it safely to where the car was parked.

The Restaurant was now entirely in flames, black smoke rising high in the sky, Drago thought of the Janitor and hoped he got out of the storeroom without too many burns.

The morning sun began to shine when Michael pulled into the underground parking of the Hotel. Both men wandered up to Drago's suite, with Michael staying only a few minutes then leaving. After a short rest, Rick ordered room service and waited for him to return.

They returned to the dock and parked across from the Restaurant, carefully avoiding the fire trucks and police out front joined by a Land Rover.

With a smirk, Rick handed Michael the binoculars.

"Take a look and tell me what you see." Rick ordered.

"One of Wong's bodyguards sitting in a car," Michael continued. "Wait a minute. Wong is here, hmm. Who is that?"

Drago took the glasses from Michael.

"That's Diana," Rick replied.

"Who is Diana?" Michael asked, squinting to look closer.

"I met her in Toronto. She's David Mercier's, daughter," Rick explained, while Michael took back the glasses.

Meanwhile Diana got into the back seat of the car with Lo Wong.

"She's getting in the back seat with Lo Wong."

"Let's go!" Rick exclaimed.

They followed the two vehicles to a large mansion outside of the city, the building surrounded by a high wall covered in green vines.

A light mist filled the morning air while the sun went behind the clouds, Michael drove by the main gate, before turning onto a side street and stopping.

There were trees along the road up against the wall ones. Rick climbed to have a better look.

Lo Wong came out of the house holding Diana's elbow as one of his men followed. Wong then got into the car after talking with her and drove away .His men led her back into the mansion.

"Do you think Wong is holding this woman hostage?" Michael asked.

"We'll soon find out," replied Drago while he lowered down from the tree.

The two men with their backs against the wall headed towards the mansion.

Rick hadn't worked with a partner since working with Joanne on his last mission to the Caribbean island of Barbados.

Drago mouth, though felt dry. He figured it might have been from the weather, somehow he felt safe working with Michael.

Rick often wondered about Joanne and how she was getting along, as last he heard she had become a field agent.

Eventually they reached the back of the building. Michael pried the old gate open and entered, checking the rooms as they went along the corridor to find them all empty.

The smell of coffee greeted them as they reached the other landing, there were two men sitting at a table having breakfast, they notice the kitchen was also very spacious in a rectangular shape with a chandelier hanging over the table, with the only light in the kitchen coming from the stove.

Rick and Michael split up moving swiftly, they caught the men by surprise, Rick covered his man's mouth with one hand as the blade found it's marked, cutting the throat from ear to ear.

Michael used the stem on his watch around the other man's neck as Rick came over and asked.

"The young lady, where is she?" Rick demanded.

"Where the hell did you come from?" asked the man. "And what the fuck you want with her?"

"You better answer me while you can, or end up like your partner over there."

"She's below," the man replied while Michael ease the tension of the wire from around the his neck.

"Where below?" Rick demanded.

"In the wine cellar, a few rooms are down there."the guard gasped, fear brewing in his eyes.

"Is she guarded?" Michael asked.

"Yes, someone's watching her."

"Is anyone else being held here?" Rick asked.

"Yes. There's a man in the room next to the woman. Please don't kill me; I'm telling you all I know!"

"Who's the man, and what's his name?" Rick Drago barked.

"I don't know his name," the guard pleaded.

"How long has he been here?" Rick Drago asked.

"He was here before I came," replied the guard.

"How many more men are here?" Rick asked.

"Three others are somewhere in the building; they're walking around checking the premises."

"The guy guarding the woman downstairs, what's his name?" Michael asked.

"His name is Thomas, and he has orders to kill anyone that tries to rescue the man or the woman, even kill the two of them if necessary."

"Where did Lo Wong go?" Drago gestured out the window.

"I don't know where he went, but he said he'd

be back in a few hours and to be ready to move out of here."

Drago shot a looked over at Michael before walking back to the guy laying on the kitchen floor, with an annoyed sigh, he began searching the man's pockets for identification.

"Are you going to kill me?" the guard in Michael's arms asked through tears.

"Of course not," Rick replied . "One more question. Do you know David Mercier? He's a Canadian."

"Yes, I do know the Canadian. Met him at the Restaurant when he came to visit Wong."

"You asked me if I was going to kill you I'm not," Drago responded, looking over at Michael. "But he is."

Michael put his knee in the center of the man's back and tightened the wire until the body went limp on the chair.

They placed the two bodies in the walk-in freezer and headed for the cellar. At the bottom of the stairs, Michael and Rick split up. Rick then saw a man coming out of a room, before locking its door. Rick turned his back, hoping the guy didn't see him.

"Who's there. Who are you?" the man asked as he approached Rick.

Suddenly the footsteps stopped as the man's body hit the floor, Rick turned and saw Michael standing over the body. Rick and Michael searched the man's pockets and found a set of keys.

"Get what information you can from him," Rick called out while heading for the locked room.

Diana was sitting at a small table inside with a pen and paper.

"Hello, Diana,"Drago said upon entering the room. She jumped out of the chair and rushed into his arms with a cry of joy.

"What," she began before Rick stopped her.

"We got to go. Do you know the person in the room next to yours?" Rick asked.

"No, I haven't seen his face, I only heard talking coming from the room," she replied as Michael came to join them.

"This is Michael Strong," Drago said introducing them to each other and handing Michael the keys. "Check the next room."

Michael then opened the door, to find a man lying on the bed rubbing his eyes.

"On your feet," Michael ordered."Time to go."

"Who are you?" the stranger asked.

"I'm your savior. On your feet man, let's get out of here before Lo Wong returns," Michael urged him up and to the door with little argument.

The four of them moved along the corridor, hearing voices causing them to stop and waited.

"Sounds like guards making their rounds," said Michael. "I'll take a look."

Moving fast in a crouch position, he came upon a door slightly ajar leading to the outside. Michael looked and saw one of the guards with a gun propped against the wall reading a magazine.

With a roll of his eyes, Michael then drew his gun and attached the silencer. He fired hitting the man in the head. Michael then yanked the body inside, hoping the other guard didn't see or hear anything.

Chapter Three

Rick and the others joined Michael, the four of them now making their way out without any more problem and eventually making it into the car.

Diana sat in the front with Michael as Rick sat in the back with the man. Only then did Rick recognize the man to be Pierre Cote. His face was much smaller and full of hair, his clothes now filthy from mistreatment.

Rick remembered the face from a photo David Mercier had shown to him. He looked like a broken man, and whatever Lo Wong had done to him was working. Diana looked back at Rick and said. "We meet again."

"Yes," Rick replied with a shrug.

"You look tired." she observed.

"And you seemed exhausted," Drago replied.

"I've been through a great deal in the past twenty-four hours," Diana gave a curt nod..

The car sped away through the morning mist, moving along the narrow country road and heading for the safe house that Michael used from his time with the Agency. Reaching the building, Michael got out and entered the building, leaving Rick and the others in the car. Minutes later Michael gave the all-clear for the rest to come in.

"Breakfast, anyone?" Michael asked.

"I'm hungry; let me help," Diana piped in.

"Who are you people?" Pierre gave a cautious look at the bunch.

"I am Rick Drago. Over there is my colleague Michael Strong and the lady is Diana Mercier; I believe you know her father."

"David Mercier is her father?" Pierre was astonished.

"Diana," Rick shouted." Meet Mr. Pierre Cote, an old friend of your dad."

She turned away from the stove and looked at Pierre.

"So, you're the one giving all this trouble," Diana mused.

"I'm not the one making all this trouble," replied Cote.

"I've been looking for you and the Prototype," Rick said.

"Did someone hired you to find me?" Pierre asked.

"I'll ask the question," Rick snapped.

"Look. Mister," Pierre began before being interrupted.

"I told you my name is Rick Drago," Rick glared.

"Mister Rick, I think David hired you to find and kill me."

"And why should he want to kill you?" Rick asked.

Pierre hesitated and began rubbing his hands together, so Drago repeated the question.

"Why should David want to kill you?"

"Because I can cause him a lot of trouble and embarrassment," replied Pierre with a shrug.

"Explain, " Rick ordered.

"You see, I'm the only one alive who knows the truth about the high-jacking of the Prototype," Pierre said looking at Rick and likely, hoping he would accept and believed his side of the story. "Do you understand what I mean?"

"Go on," Rick gave a dismissive wave. "I'm listening."

"I was told to take some time off until the

investigation finished; I knew something like this takes a long time, and now someone wants me to take the fall for the holdup," Pierre admitted.

"Who wanted you to take the fall?" Rick Drago asked.

"After being at home trying to put the pieces of this puzzle together, I decide to take a trip to Europe. One day out of the blue, David shows up at my Hotel suite saying he saw me getting on the elevator and came up to say hello."

"You didn't believe him?" Rick asked.

"Of course not, how did he know where I was staying unless he had me followed?" Pierre continued "After listening to him, I'm convinced he was the mastermind behind the high-jacking, and what he has done I should have done."

"What's that?" Rick asked.

"I should have hired a detective,"Pierre said.

"I'm not a detective," Rick replied.

"Then, what are you?"

"Go on with the story."

"David did his part, and I think something went wrong at the exchanged, so now he thinks I have the Prototype or at least know where it is."

"Do you?"

"No, I don't and never did, may I have a cigarette?" Pierre now looked nervous.

"I don't smoke."

Pierre cote began rubbing his hands together, eyes looking at the floor, and squeezing his knuckles until they turned white.

"Tell me more about this meeting in your suite," Rick said.

Pierre raised his head and looked Rick in his eyes and said.

"I accused him of masterminding the heist and do you know what he said to me. You're the one on record of not doing your duty and making sure that the shipment reached the destination safely. So I told him that he was lying."

"Go on," Rick ordered, Pierre didn't seem very happy to do so as sweat trickled on his forehead.

"I told him only two people knew the route and time. I didn't mention it to anyone, which left only you. He began walking in the room, then said. "How much would it take?" I am an old man, they made me an offer and threatened my family. I had no choice." Pierre finally said.

"Did you tell him what it would cost to keep your mouth shut?" Rick Drago asked.

"I gave him a figure of 200.000 American dollars and a couple of days to have it ready, and he left."

"After the meeting, what did you do?"

"I sat in my suite thinking, then decided to pay my bill and get out of the hotel, but when I got back to my suite, two men were waiting for me. I've been held captive from that day until you found me."

Rick wondered why David asked him to find Pierre when he already knew the man was being held captive by Lo Wong. Maybe it was a double-cross by the people looking for the Prototype.

Rick thought to himself, then asked."Did the men that took you ever ask you about the Prototype?"

"No, it's like after. They weren't sure what to do with me, they then received a call , and then they took me to that place where you found me," Pierre replied.

"I think your friend David is in trouble with these people. I also believed he doesn't know you've been kidnap, and the kidnappers also took his daughter. "Have you met her before?"

"No. This is the first time we've met," Pierre replied.

"Do you think that David would have you kidnapped, then do the same thing to his daughter?" Rick asked.

"No, I don't believe he would do that," Pierre Cote said.

After the conversation with Pierre. He wanted to know if David was her biological father or dad by marriage.

Rick went to talk with Diana he turned the door handle and opened it slowly.

Michael and Diana were lying in bed. "Hmm, you're so big and sweet, I want you to fill me," Diana said to Michael.

Rick closed the door without hesitation and went back to Pierre.

Rick now believed that David wanted Pierre found so he could shut him up. The man had betrayed the people he worked for, after all, and his close friends and his sex-starved daughter had become a pawn in the game.

"What are you going to do?" Pierre asked.

"You'll have to stay here for another day or two. Lo Wong will have his people looking for you and Diana," Rick Drago replied with a sigh.

"I understand. I'll do what you say." Pierre agreed.

A few minutes later, Michael and Diana walked into the room.

"Diana, I want to have a word with you," Drago stated.

"A word," said Michael now looking at Rick.

The two men left Diana and Pierre in the room alone.

"David Mercier sent Diana here to talk with Lo Wong, something about investing in the Hotel business," Michael said to Drago.

"What! Shouted Drago, turning and began

heading back to the room where Diana and Pierre were waiting.

"I think my dad has betrayed many people, including me," Diana said.

"Is David your biological father?" Rick asked.

"No, he married my mom when my sister and I were teens. We took his name after the adoption. Eighteen years ago David met my mom. Six weeks later they got married," Diana explained.

The telephone rang and Michael picked up the receiver. "Hello?"

"You don't know me, but we must meet. I know you're not alone. I will call again,"the voice on the other line said.

"Who is this?" asked Michael, before the line went dead.

"What's wrong?" Rick demanded.

"Someone knows they're here and wants to have a talk with me," Michael looked at the two they'd rescued.

"I gather that caller didn't leave a name or number?"

"No, it didn't," Michael sighed.

"The voice was it oriental?"

"No, it sound English. Had no accent." Michael explained.

"We have to get out of here!" Rick exclaimed.

"Let's go then" Michael taking a key from the

house key-ring and insert it into a slot in one of the draws in the kitchen. Almost immediately a door in the wall opened to reveal a lift, they got into the lift, and a few seconds later they were deep under the building.

"How deep are we?" Diana looked around in wonder.

"About twenty feet down," Michael said, as he opened the car door. "This road runs about five miles underground and comes out near the heart of London there's only two entries, and we controls them both."

Michael then booted the car along the narrow underground road, soon reaching the safe house in the heart of London.

Diana and Pierre were left guarded by Michael's people. This place served as Michael's office of operation as well as the safe house.

A note was waiting for Rick at the hotel reception desk. He read it then handed the note to Michael.

"How do you want to play this?" Michael asked after reading it.

The note read. *David Mercier is missing, please wait in your room until contacted!*

Both men looked around the lobby. Rick then turned and asked the receptionist. "Did you receive this message?"

"No, Sir, it was here when I came on duty,"

the receptionist replied.

"No one told you who delivered it?" Drago questioned.

"No, Sir."

"Let's have a drink," Drago commanded as he turned to heads towards the bar with Michael trailing behind. They sat at a corner booth.

"David is missing, looks like the other side is winning," Michael said.

"Not for long," replied Drago. "The kid gloves are off."

"Why would they do that to David?" Michael asked.

"Don't know, but the person that delivered that note has to be here still. They have to report when I arrived back at the hotel."

"How was she?" Rick suddenly blurted.

The question caught Michael by surprise.

"The same as her sister;" Michael continued. "Yes. She told me about you and her sister. It seems they're very close and tell each other everything."

"It looks as if David tried to double-cross the wrong people and got himself into trouble." Rick said trying to changed the subject.

"Are you going to your room to wait to be contacted?" Michael asked after a few moments of quiet between them.

"No, I never play by the opposition rules, if

you do, you'll never win," Rick shrugged.

"Then, I'll go to your room if anyone should follow," Michael didn't have to finish the sentence; Rick knew what he meant. He stayed seated and watched as Michael got on the elevator.

Rick ordered another Jack Daniel. Five minutes later, Rick got up, went to the and used the hotel phone and called his suite; he knew something was wrong when Michael didn't answer.

Rick took the elevator, got off on the floor below his suite and took the stairs the rest of the way. The door to his suite was open.

The room was a mess. It looked like a hurricane had passed through it.

Michael had to have put up a fight, so at least he was still alive, Rick put the no disturb sign on the door and hurried along the corridor before asking the nearby housekeeper if she had seen a big guy about his size.

"Yes," she replied. "That man was in the company of three Oriental looking people. They nearly knocked me over as they passed by."

So it took three of them to knock out Michael. Rick thought to himself. He followed the pointed finger of the housekeeper, to the service elevator, the light showing it was on the fifth floor.

Rick took the next available elevator down to

the main level and rushed out of the hotel. He then found the Jaguar hoping that Michael had a spare set of keys somewhere in the car.

Drago searched and found a set of keys in the ash-tray. Next, he started the car and waited at the entrance to the underground parking.

Not knowing what kind of vehicle they would be taking Michael in, he decided to follow the first one to come out of the lot.

Minutes later, the sound of tires burning rubber greeted his ears when a car came racing out of the garage.

Rick started to follow. He kept a few car lengths back as they headed for the expressway, Rick decided to take a closer look at who was inside the vehicle.

Rick came alongside, and saw two men sat in the front seat. Michael sat in the back between two other men, his head slump forward.

They might have drugged Michael. Rick thought to himself as he slowed the Jaguar, letting the other car move ahead, the next exit sign read 'London Docks.'

The driver took the exit as Rick got boxed in the lane. He then maneuvered to the inside lane and onto the shoulder, coming to a stop.

Putting the car in reverse. Rick backed up until the car reached the ramp for the exit, the Jaguar roaring with a burst of speed as Rick floored the gas pedal.

Reaching the docks, Rick found the abandoned car, and saw a fishing trawler pulling out of the harbor. Michael was gone. Then the phone in the car began to ring. Rick picked up the receiver with an annoyed huff.

"You will find that Prototype and deliver it to me personally if you ever want to see your friend again,"the voice on the other end commanded.

"If you," Drago began to say, before being interrupted.

"You're in no position to make any threats to me, although these idiots that work for me made a mistake and brought me the wrong person. Mr.Drago, I will call again."

The phone went dead; and Rick drove back to the safe house where Diana and Pierre were waiting.

He then put a call through to the General and explained the latest developments.

"What happened to David? " Rick demanded.

"Nothing. What do you mean?" the General seemed surprised he'd asked.

"Can you get your hands on the sample model of the Prototype?" Rick asked.

"Maybe, What's going on?" General Applewaite queried.

"Lo Wong is holding Michael and won't release him until I bring him the Prototype. His men made a mistake and took him when they were supposed to grab me instead," Drago replied.

"Okay, I will make a few calls and get back to you," General Applewaite said before hanging up.

Rick then ran a check on the fishing trawler named Lin Wing and found the boat to be registered in Bermuda.

"Where is Michael?" Diana asked.

"He's gone on a trip," Drago replied. "And we leave tomorrow."

"Where did he go?" Diana asked.

"He'll tell you when the time is right," Drago shrugged.

"I tried to reach my Dad, but couldn't," she said . "You and Pierre will fly to Toronto and will be met at the airport by General Applewaite security people, this is for your safety,"Rick said "Both of you were kidnapped before, and the same people may try to do it again.

"What about you?" she asked .

"I am going to Bermuda."

"Will I ever see you again?"

"If I'm ever in Toronto again, I will be sure to look you up," Rick promised.

Reaching forward, Diana kissed Rick on the

cheek, before whispering in his ear. "I know about you and my sister." with that she walked away, swinging her hips with every step.

The call from the General came later that evening. He assured Rick that the sample would be available in twenty-four hours.

Rick then told the General about the trawler registration, and that he was going to Bermuda to check on it. He said he'd contact the General with information on where to send the prototype sample.

Thirty six hours later, Rick was in a Limo heading through the streets of Bermuda.

The General made all the arrangements in Bermuda for Rick Drago and send the information to him. The name on the paper read 'Wheatmore'.

They would be happy to accommodate you, and give you any assistant you may need. A car will be waiting for you at the airport.

His car then stopped at the gate to the stately mansion.

"This is it," said the driver, waiting for the gates to be open. A woman was waiting to greet him at the door when Rick exited the car.

"The Wheatmore's are expecting me," Rick told her.

"Yes, do come in, Mr. Drago." she gestures inside.

Rick entered, taking a quick look at the spacious room, beautiful art pieces hanging on the walls, well-polished furniture, and rugs on the floor.

Rick didn't see the two men who entered the room behind him until he turned. They were well equipped, clean-cut and smartly dressed, with a nod from the woman they disappeared as quickly and quietly as they had appeared.

"I am Maggie Wheatmore. Welcome to my home." the woman introduced herself with shake of hands.

"Thank you," replied Rick while he walked with her into another room.

"Do you have anything for me?"

"That depends on what you're talking about. I have many things," Maggie replied.

"A package, or a message?" Rick asked.

"Relax Mr. Drago. Everything in due time, the package you seek will be here tomorrow. In the meantime, I think you should rest. Your room is upstairs, the first door on the left." she nodded up the stairs.

Rick picked up his only piece of luggage before heading for the stairs. "You seem to be well informed," he said to Maggie Wheatmore.

"Take a look at the screen," Maggie said.

Rick watched while his photo appeared along with his height, weight, and age. "You see Mr.Drago; I know everything about you."

Rick looked at her in shock. "Everything?"

"Yes, and I do mean everything. Now go get some rest, and I'll see you after you've freshened up."

Rick Drago headed up to the second floor, eventually reaching his room. He vanished inside his bedroom knowing she had been watching his every move, the thought disturb him as did the idea of her watching his butt when he went up the stairs.

The house butler woke Rick at six in the evening. The Madam is waiting for you downstairs. You will wear a jacket when you join her," said the butler when he left the room.

Rick took a shower and got dress; Twenty minutes later, he was heading down the stairs, to find the butler waiting for him. "Follow me, Sir!" ordered the butler as he turned and led the way.

Rick then followed the man through an archway that led to a room with two massive doors which swung open with ease. The smell of expensive perfume and the aroma of pipe smoke, filled the air.

Sitting on a sofa that nearly took up the length of the room were Maggie and two other women, while two distinguish looking men stood at the bar sipping drinks from tall glasses.

Maggie stood up when Rick entered the room. "Everyone, this is Mr. Rick Drago, the man I've been telling you all about,"Maggie quickly slid her hand under Rick's arm.

"Am I supposed to be your lover or friend?" Rick in the lowest voice he could muster.

She didn't have time to answer as the two men stepped forward.

"I am General Wally Wheatmore. It's a pleasure to meet you," said the taller of the two men, shaking Rick's hand with a firm grip. Rick returned a little pressure of his own.

"This is my Dad," Maggie said as the General and Rick Drago continued shaking hands..

"And I am General Theodore Saulsby," the other man announced with an outstretched hand.

"Pleasure," Rick Drago nodded shaking General Saulsby hand.

Maggie led Drago to where the two women sat.

"This is my Dad's wife. Elaine," Maggie said.

The woman was sitting with her back to Rick when he entered the room. Now, for the first time, he saw her face. Drago gently shook her hand; it seemed like their eyes locked onto each other for a long time.

"And this is Vivian Saulsby," Maggie said gesturing to the other woman.

"You haven't answered my question," Rick Drago sigh.

"What was the question?" Maggie queried.

Chapter Four

After introductions, Rick Drago went and joined the men at the bar. Maggie sat with the women on the sofa.

Rick admired the two Generals and the shape they were in, having two wives much younger than they are, both women beautiful and stunning.

A few minutes later, the butler announced that dinner was ready to be served. Maggie's dad and his wife sat at the head of the table. Rick sat next to Maggie, and General Saulsby and his wife sat on the other side.

After dinner, everyone had dessert, with a few cocktails before retiring to their rooms.

Early the next morning, the butler called Rick Drago to the phone.

"Mr. Rick , please," said the voice on the other end of the line.

"This is Rick. who is this?" he asked.

"Mr. Rick Drago, you're a very elusive man and I like that. You have proven more than once, that you're a worthy adversary. Perhaps one day we can work together for the same cause."

Rick had heard similar words when he was in London.

"And what cause would that be?" Drago asked the voice on the other end of the line.

"Not to be dominated by one man or one country. as you know, the price for that can be very high both in money and human life," the voice said.

"How can I help you? And what shall I call you?" Rick asked.

"You have something that belongs to me. When can you deliver it?"

"I'm afraid you're mistaken. I don't have anything for you," Rick replied.

"Mr. Rick Drago. You won't be doing any more business with Lo Wong. He worked for me, and I'm afraid he's no longer among the living."the comment sent shivers done Rick Drago's spine.

Drago thought about Lo Wong and the many mistakes he'd made.

What with the Restaurant In London, England going up in flames. The house in the country where they kept Pierre Cote, and Diana Mercier. Causing the lives of his men, eventually losing his own.

"It is I who has your friend from London, and unless you co-operate with me, there's no telling what will happen to him." the voice on the other end broke the eerie silence that had settled over Rick.

"How do I know what you're saying is true?" Rick asked.

"I won't try to fool a man like you, I know of your reputation, in my circle they call you the Destructor, a man of many talents."

Rick smiled. He had been called the fixer, the hunter, the master of the kill, the death provider, but never the Destructor.

"Let me speak to him. I want proof of life."

"In due time." said the man.

"Where shall we meet?" Rick questioned.

"I have a house in the country not far from the city. Shall we say noon tomorrow," And Mr. Rick Drago, please bring the item with you. If not I may become very disappointed and take action on your friend."

"I'll be there," Rick snapped before hanging up the phone.

Turning around, he saw that Maggie was approaching.

"We've got the location," she said, handing Rick a piece of paper with an address on it.

"We have all the latest tech knowledge here. Listening, tracking, you name it, we have it. Follow me," Maggie ordered as she pushed the center of her belt buckle, revealing a door.

The butler and the driver were sitting at a big desk with many controls.

"This is our brain here, and that call came from this location," Maggie said pointing at a place on the map of the local area.

"I'll check that place after dark," Rick replied with a nod.

"They will go with you," Maggie suggested indicating the driver and the butler.

Midnight and Rick were ready to go hunting, the butler, and the driver was waiting for him.

Maggie gave Rick a listening device for his ear. A short time later, they arrived at the address.

"Four people inside," Rick could hear Maggie's voice. "One person is sitting, one standing at the door, the other two at a table."

Rick, the driver and the butler, decided to enter from the back, not wanting to crash through the front and give the guards a chance to kill Michael.

It was over so quickly that the guards didn't have much time to react.

"What kept you?" asked Michael while Rick untied him from the chair.

"Had to make a few stops along the way," said Drago. "Guys, this is Michael."

The men shook hands with the captive. One of the guards was still alive, and Rick decided to try and get information from him before he passed out.

The Guard didn't know much about what was going on, as he was only on the job for the last two days.

Fifteen minutes later, they were back at Maggie's place. She had a room prepared for Michael, thinking he was severely hurt.

Michael has a busted lip, and bruises around his right eye.

"Maggie, this is Michael. He came from London to meet you," Drago said taking Michael to the room Maggie had prepared for him..

Michael and Maggie shook hands as she touches his face, examining his busted lip and the bruises around his eye.

"I'll be alright,"Michael brushed her off.

"You two guys should clean up and get some rest, tomorrow is going to be a busy day for all of us," Maggie ordered before turning to walk away swinging her hips with every step, and giving Rick and Michael precisely what they wanted to see.

Suddenly she stopped and turned, with a big smile on her face, looking at both of them, and then entered her room.

The next day Rick along with Maggie's two associates, along with Michael, arrived at the planned meeting place. Michael stayed in the SUV while Rick and the others went into the house.

After speaking with a man dressed in a uniform, they walked back to the SUV and informed Michael that the owner had left earlier that morning.

Rick decided to visit the place where they held Michael captive.

"I wonder what happen to the ones who were guarding me," Michael asked.

"They'll meet the same fate as Lo Wong," Rick Drago.

Arriving at the place where Michael was held captive, they realize it was only a few minutes from the house where the meeting was to take place.

The damaged windows and doors had been replaced with new ones. The broken furniture was gone, and the room was tidy and clean as if nothing had happened.

Rick Drago and the others search the rooms, while Michael took the fire-place looking for any clues as to where to find the owner. They found nothing and were about to leave and go back to Maggie's house.

Michael was searching through the ash where they burn the papers, when suddenly, a crumpled wet piece of paper caught his eye. He picked it up and carefully opened the article.

"Hey guys, look what I found," Michael called out.

Parts of the paper letter-head were missing, as was the full name of the shipping, but the location read. Port au Prince Haiti.

"Let's go,"Rick ordered.

Maggie was on the steps to greet them. Michael simply gave her the piece of paper he found. She went back into her office.

"Rick Drago. You leave tomorrow morning for Haiti, " Maggie declared.

"Well, old buddy, guess you'll be heading back to England," Rick chuckled looking at Michael.

"I'm going to stay a few more days and enjoy this beautiful Island and all it has to offer before heading to old foggy London," Michael replied, looking at Maggie while she turned and walk away.

"Yes. I know what you mean. Wish I could stay longer, but duty calls and I must obey. There's lots here to enjoy," Rick shrugged.

"I'll make a few calls, then go for a walk on the beach," Michael nodded.

The two men didn't have to say anything more to each other. For the little time they've been together, a bond had formed between the two that only operatives in the field would know about..

After supper and a few cocktails, Maggie went to her room and left the men chatting. Michael wanted to go out and visit a nightclub, but Rick talked him out of going.

A few hours later, the men called it a night and went to their room. Rick had decided to pack his things, and he noticed a small opening at the back of the clothes closet, Rick Drago pushed and a door open, before stepping into a large bedroom. On the bed was a black satin sheet and under that a form of a body.

Rick moved swiftly and silently to the side of the bed, he removed the sheet revealing the body of Maggie. He then turn her head and place his hand over her mouth. She quickly wrapped her arms around his neck with a sigh.

"I was just thinking about you," Maggie said. "What took you so long?"

Rick covered her mouth with his, passionately kissing her. He found her breast as the nipples became hard, sucking on them Maggie moaned with delight.

His hands were exploring the rest of her body, fondling and caressing.

Maggie parted her legs, waiting for that touch. She waited for his hands to find and explore her most precious belonging. She felt the wetness on her legs.

Rick entered her. He Thrust his rod deep into her, and she matched his rhythm while pure delight erupted from her mouth.

Lying in each other arms after the lovemaking, then the phone in Maggie's room rang, she answered.

"Madam, the Professor Sir James Conrad, is

here to see you," said the butler.

Drago went back to his room the same way he had entered Maggie's bedroom. A few minutes later, she knocked on his door.

"Sir James would like to have a few words with you," Maggie said. Her stunning body was showing every curve beneath the gown she was wearing.

Rick got dressed and followed her to the room where the Professor Sir James Conrad was waiting. He sat at the only table occupying the room.

"I received a call from a good friend of mine; General Applewaite. I believed you know him?" Sir James asked.

"Yes, I know him," Rick replied.

"He insisted that I speak with you before you leave for Haiti, and fill you in on what I know." Sir James said.

"Thanks for coming," Rick Drago shook his hand.

Sir James looked at Maggie. "Now, my dear, you'll have to excuse yourself and leave us! You're more beautiful than your mother."

Maggie did as Sir James asked and left the room, closing the door behind her.

"If I were still a young man, I'd go after that

prize," he laughed.

"Yes, she's a good one, alright," Rick nodded.

Taking a picture from his pocket, Sir James began looking and turning it, then handed it to Drago.

"She's beautiful isn't she?" he asked

"Yes, she sure is beautiful."Rick Drago admitted eyeing her over.

"My wife, " said Sir James.

"I haven't much time before I leave for *Haiti*," Rick Drago said.

"I think you should sit down; this will take more than a few minutes. All this began when I was working at the university in Canada. My colleague and I started to create a machine that would be capable of extracting the salt from the ocean waters and pumping out clean water," said Sir James as he began taking a sip of water.

"We discovered, that not only was it capable of removing the salt. But it could be useful for other things too."

"Things, such as what?" Rick Drago raised a brow.

"With a few adjustments, it could track a stealth plane and in the wrong hands bring that plane down. Keeping something that big was very hard to do, and my colleague was thinking about the Nobel prize. I tried to explain to him that they won't give a Nobel prize for something this monstrous,"Sir James gave an exasperated sigh.

"How did he take it?"

"Not very well. He took time off from the University. The last I heard, he was driving along the country road in *Newfoundland* and went over a cliff, supposedly he died at the scene."

"What happened after that?" Rick Drago asked.

"The story broke about him making this surprising discovery and wanted to sell the information on the black market. He and I had decided we would keep a different section of our development on our laptop. After his death, I removed the hard drive from his computer and destroyed it," Sir James said.

"And your section, where is it?" Rick Drago asked.

"I still have it," Sir James replied.

"Who else knows about this?" Rick Drago asked.

"It's a closely guarded secret," said the professor. "After the death of my colleague, I was invited to meet with someone at a place of my choosing, so I decided on the cafeteria at the school."

"Go on!" Rick gave an impatient wave of his hand.

"The man I met showed me a video of a car

burning with people inside; He explained to me that it was my family and warned me to cooperate with them, or the same thing will happen to me. I immediately tried to reach my wife and kids, but couldn't,"Sir James said.

"Did you inform the police?" Rick asked.

"Yes, I contacted the cops."

"Did you tell them about the meeting?"

"No, I told them that my wife drives a car like the one that was burning with people inside, and I can't reach her.

They explained that the crash was so violent and in such a difficult place to reach, dental records would have to be used to identify the bodies inside the burnt-out car.

"You mentioned children, how many do you have?" Rick inquired.

"They were two girls, Diana and Charlotte; They perish in that car with their mother." Sir James said.

"So. Did you got the confirmation from the authorities about the bodies in the car?"

"Yes."

"Were you contacted again by the person that showed you the video of the car burning?"

"No, I immediately resigned, disconnected my phone, took the ashes they gave to me of my family and returned to *England*. I also changed my name, and made a little alteration on my nose," Sir James replied.

"I'll be back in a moment," said Rick when he got up from his seat and left the room.

Rick went in search of Maggie and found her in the communication room.

"I need photos of David Mercier, Lo Wong, and Pierre Cote,"Rick Drago ordered.

"How's the old man doing?" Maggie asked.

"How long have you known him?"Rick asked.

"Many, many years," she said.

"What about his wife. Did you know her?"

"Yes. I know he lost his wife a long time ago, no more than that. Why do you ask?" queried Maggie.

"I just wanted to know how much you know of his family,"Rick shrugged.

"The photos will be ready in a few minutes," Maggie said.

Rick waited until the photos were printed out. Then, he took the pictures and returned to the room where Sir James was waiting; He showed the photos to Sir James.

"Do you recognize any of these men?" Rick asked the professor.

Sir James looked at the three photos, then took the one of David Mercier.

"It was so long ago, but this one there's something about the face. Maybe I saw him in a magazine somewhere."

Rick took the picture from Sir James and left the room. A few minutes later, he returned with a copy of a younger David Mercier and handed it to Sir James.

"Yes, that's the man I met in the cafeteria; he's the one who showed me the video of those people burning in the car."

"Are you sure this is the man?"Rick Drago queried.

"Yes, that's him; I'm positive." Who is he?" Sir James asked.

"His name is David Mercier," Rick replied.

"They wanted me to betray my adoptive country Canada, and I wouldn't have any part of it even after they threatened me," Sir James said.

"Have you been approached by anyone since you moved here?" Rick Drago questioned.

"No, but I've heard rumors about members of the "C.M.L.F". "Communism Must Live Forever." trying to find anyone with information on a retired professor and offering reward money," Sir James said.

Rick wanted to tell the older man that the ashes he took back to *England* weren't his family; his wife and daughters were still alive and living with David Mercier.

The wife and children receive the news about his death on a fishing trip, and the body hasn't been recovered yet.

"What can you tell me about the assistants that worked with you?" Rick asked.

"My colleague and I had one bright young man each, working with us."

"Do you think either one of them could've sold copies of your work to anyone?"

"I never thought about the young men; I always thought it might've been my colleague," the Professor trailed off.

"Do you remember their names; The young men that assist you and your colleague in the lab?" Rick Drago asked.

"I would have to log-in to the university to get their names. I don't even know if my password is still active, and if it is, they would trace it back to me. Maggie could help you with that, she can hack into the university computer easily," the Professor said.

"Anything else you remember about the meeting you had with David in the cafeteria?"

"He had mentioned that the group had many members in high places above suspicion in many countries," Sir James said after a moment of thought.

"Is it possible that someone hacked into your computer?" Rick raised a brow.

"I suppose someone could've gotten paid to do that, maybe a student. Some of them are good at doing such things," Sir James replied.

Rick Drago sat down for the first time since entering the room; Sir James was right when he said it would take more than a few minutes.

"I believe that they approached my colleague about our work, and he turned them down. Then they killed him when he vacationed in Newfoundland, next it was me, showing me pictures of my family to make me sell them information."

"I have to leave soon, so I'll ask Maggie to run a check. I'll need the year of birth and the full name of your colleague!" .

Sir James wrote the information down on a piece of paper and handed it over.

After listening to Sir James tell the story of a dream he had about his family and a few more details of what he did after retiring from the university, Rick got up and shook the older man's hand, he'd heard enough from Sir James.

"David Mercier. Mr. Drago, do you know this person?" Sir James asked.

"Yes, our paths have crossed," Rick Drago replied.

"The plans you're carrying are genuine. So is the prototype you received from General Applewaite" Sir James assured Rick Drago.

Rick began to walk towards the door; before going out, he stopped and turned to face the older man with a questionable look on his face.

"Yes; They are. I should know my work when I see it."

"Earlier, you told me that you have your section of the work, where is it?" Rick asked.

"The box is in London," Sir James said.

"When was the last time you checked it?" Rick asked.

"It's been quite some time; the rental fees automatically come from my account."

"So, these papers are a copy of your work and not the original?" Rick asked.

"Yes, let me explain. I was asked by a group of influential people to help them create a prototype to bring the members of "C.M.L.F." out in the open. There was a copy made and the prototype created, that's the package that you received from Applewaite," Sir James responded.

"I'll be leaving early in the morning; Maggie will forward any information she finds on the young men who assisted you with your work in the lab at the university. Goodbye, Sir James." Rick Drago finally said.

"You're not taking her with you? she could be a great help to you, fluent in many languages. Do you speak french or creole?" Sir James asked.

"Yes, I speak French."

"Okay, but you don't have to let Maggie know. I think she would like to go with you if asked, I see the way you both look at each other," Sir

James laugh.

The time was seven in the morning; Rick woke up from the shaking of Michael's hand on his shoulder.

"What time is it?" he groaned.

"Seven in the morning, time for you to get going! I think the host was waiting to have breakfast with you."

"I have no time for breakfast," Rick Drago said heading into the bathroom.

"What time is your flight?" Michael asked.

"Nine, I'd like you to find out where Diana is, and you should know she's the biological daughter of Sir James."

Michael left the room and went in search of Maggie. "Can I have a secure line to London? "he asked.

Maggie took him to an office, took up the phone and entered in a few numbers, before handing the phone to him. Michael dialed his office number in London.

"Hello," said the man's voice on the other end of the receiver.

"Still lost, " replied Michael as he waited to hear the familiar clicks.

"MS One, we thought you were dead. The search for your body is still going on as we speak," the man on the line known as E.E by his fellow operatives, gasped.

"Not dead, I'm very much alive. Where are Diana and Pierre?" Michael asked.

"After arriving in Canada, Diana took a flight to Montreal"

"What about Pierre?" Michael demanded.

"The police found his body in a hotel room outside of Toronto."

"Diana, is she still in Montreal?"

"As of late last night, yes, she's still there." E.E said.

"I'll be back in a couple of days, so continue to keep Diana under surveillance, I want to know every move she makes and who she sees!" commanded Michael.

Along paused at the other end of the line.

"Will do, and we'll call off the search for your missing body," said the operative, with a laugh.

"I'll pass this information on to Rick," Michael said.

"Where's Mr. Drago?" E.E asked.

"He's here with me and will be leaving shortly for Haiti. Do you know Sir James Conrad?"

"Yes, I do," E.E replied.

"Am I right with the assumption that you're the one responsible for him being in the Caribbean?" Michael asked.

A pause. "Yes, Sir James and I go a long way back. Is he dead?" the operative asked.

"No, he's very much alive," Michael replied.

"He had a little too much on his mind, so I suggested he go to Bermuda. We both have friends living there," E.E said.

"We found out that his family is not dead. The "C.M.L.F" wanted him to believe they perished in the burnt-out car."

"Does he know?" E.E asked.

"No, Rick thinks it's best not to let him know at this time; He'll inform him when everything is over."

"Where is his family?" the operative questioned.

"You remember Diana?"

"Yes, I do. She's a beautiful young lady."

"Diana is the younger of Sir James's daughters, and Rick wants all the information we gather to be pass on to General Applewaite."

"The General is already up to date; our friends in Canada have David Mercier under twenty-four hours surveillance." E.E responded.

Chapter Five

By the time Michael finished with his call, Rick was ready to travel. Michael walked with him while he headed for the limo that would take him to the private airstrip for his flight to Haiti. He then informed Rick about the latest developments with Diana and Pierre.

"They were supposed to be met at the Toronto airport by the General security people. What is she doing in Montreal?" Drago asked.

"I'll let you know as things come about,"

Michael said.

"And Pierre?"

"I understand they missed the flight from London to Canada and had to book new flights, Diana went on to Montreal, and Pierre was picked up at the airport. He was taken to a hotel and a few days later they found his body,"Michael said.

They both shook hands; Rick then got into the back seat of the limo as Michael turned and walked back into the house. Sitting in the car was Maggie.

"You were going to leave without saying goodbye?" Maggie demanded.

"What makes you think that this is goodbye?" asked Rick when the vehicle pulled away from the house.

"Here's your diplomatic credentials and the name of your contact who will be meeting you on arrival," said Maggie with sadness in her voice as she handed Rick an attache case.

Two hours later, Rick stepped off the plane in Haiti, waiting for him was a tall red haired young woman.

"Mr. Rick. I'm Jane Blackwell."she offered a wave.

"Please call me, Rick!"

"You have an appointment tomorrow at noon with Mr. Ling, " Jane said as she took him through the VIP section of the airport. Rick showed his diplomatic credentials and was wave on through.

"Who arranged the meeting, and where is it's going to be?" Rick asked while walking with Jane to her car.

"I'll accompany you to the meeting; it will take place at the social club name. "The Crow."

Thirty minutes later. The car stopped in front of the Hotel. "This is where you'll be staying," Jane announced as she opened the door got out, and began walking to the hotel entrance with Rick close behind.

Reaching the front desk, she asked for the keys to Rick's suite, on the ride in the elevator she began to check Drago out looking at him from head to toe whiles Rick pretended not to notice.

Jane then handed Rick the key card to his suite and began to turn away.

"Where is this social club? And what are you doing tonight? I want to visit this place," he blurted out.

"Are you asking me out?" Jane asked with wide eyes.

"If you don't want to go, I'll understand, since you're just now meeting me for the first time. But I don't want to walk in there, not knowing anything about the place."

"Okay, what time?" Jane cocked her head curiously.

"You know the Island better than I do," Rick Drago shrugged.

"I'll pick you up at eleven tonight," Jane said with a smile.

"Eleven it is. See you then," Rick Drago watched Jane as she turned and walked to the elevator with a sway in her body.

At ten-thirty at night, Rick got dressed and went downstairs to sit at the bar; he ordered a Jack Daniels neat, and a few minutes later Jane entered the room and sat beside him. She wore a sleeveless tight fitting fishtail flowered cocktail dress, showing all the curves of her body.

"Shall we go?" Jane said.

"Lead on!" Rick gave a nervous laugh.

"Good evening, Miss Blackwell," said the doorman when Jane and Rick reach the entrance to the club.

"Good evening George," Jane replied.

The matre'd took them to a table.

"It's nice to see you again, Miss Jane." he said pulling a chair out for Jane to sit.

"Nice to see you too, Vincent," Jane flashed an innocent smile.

"I'll send the waiter over!" with that he was gone.

"I take it; you're a regular at this place," Rick

observed.

"About eight months, from the time I arrived on the Island, we've got this place under surveillance." she shrugged.

"And the staff, especially the doorman George?" Rick asked.

"He's one of us; he got the job six months ago when the other doorman was seriously hurt, and yes, I'm a regular client at least once a week."

"Do you know the owner too?" Rick Drago asked.

"I've never met the owner, but I know the manager, he's sitting at the table close to the entrance," Jane said gesturing to him with a nod of her head. "Wearing a white suit and hat."

"And the meeting? Do you know the person who I'll be meeting?" Rick asked.

"I've never Mr. Ling Sahig. We believe he's the owner of "The Crow" social club," Jane said.

After having a couple of drinks and checking the entrances and exit doors, Drago and Jane left the social club, they got into the car and Jane drove Rick back to his hotel.

"I'll pick you up in the morning, say eleven-thirty," said Jane stopping the car in front of the hotel where Rick is staying.

"You're not coming up for a nightcap?" Rick asked.

"No, you should get some rest, I know of your

reputation, and I'm flattered," said Jane looking into Rick's face without so much as a smile.

"Until tomorrow," Rick chuckled as he exited the car.

He stood on the steps of the hotel. And watched as the rear lights of the Mercedes disappeared into the night.

From the hotel suite, Rick put through a call to *Bermuda* using the cell phone he got from Maggie.

"Hi, Rick. Is everything alright?" she asked after picking up the phone.

"Yes, I just returned from the club where the meeting is to take place, and Jane will be going with me tomorrow," Rick said.

"She's beautiful, isn't she?" asked Maggie.

"Yes, she is," Rick said simply.

"I trained her; Please don't let anything happen to her!"

"I gather you, and she is very close," he observed.

"Yes, we are. Jane is my niece."

"I thought I saw some resemblance between the two of you," Rick said.

"And Rick, please don't! Maggie exclaimed.

"I know Maggie, but I can't make any promises. I'll try very hard, not to, but she's gorgeous."

"Okay,"she said defeated.

"Is Michael close? I'll like to speak with him," said Drago.

"Yes, he's here," Maggie replied handing the phone over to Michael.

"You should take Sir James back to England with you!" Rick suggested."What day are you planning to leave?"

"A couple more days and I'll be on my way back to London. I'll take him back with me. As it turns out, Sir James has friends in many different places," Michael chuckled.

"What do you mean?"

"Sir James and one of my colleagues are very close; my colleague is responsible for him being here in Bermuda, and he's the one that suggested to Sir James to came and relax down here."

"Anyhow, Michael. "I got to go and get some rest, a big day tomorrow," Rick Drago yawned.

"Okay, I'll keep you informed about the movements of Diana," Michael said before the line went dead.

Rick Drago then went to bed for a much needed rest.

A knock on the door came just as Rick Drago was exiting the shower.

He wrapped a towel around his waist and opened the door. Standing there was Jane Blackwell, sunglasses tucked on her forehead.

"Come in!" Rick said "I'm just now getting

out of the shower."

"Yes, I can see you're not ready," Jane replied curtly before stepping into the room and closing the door.

Rick took a boxer under-wear from his bag and entered the bathroom. Moments later, he walked back into his room and began to dress. He also noticed Jane's eyes were staring at the bulge in his underwear.

"Are we going to have lunch at the Crow Club?" he asked .

Jane seemed to be thinking about something else as she didn't answer the question until Rick Drago asked a second time.

"Yes, I made a reservation for us," Jane finally said, blushing.

"Shall we go?" Rick asked gesturing to the door.

"Uh, yeah. Let's go."

On the ride down in the elevator, Jane stood in a corner while Rick turned to faced her.

"May I ask what you were thinking about in the room?" Rick asked as he now stands very close in front of her.

"I Was thinking about what could go wrong at this meeting," Jane replied, mouth stuck in a tight line.

"What do you think could go wrong? Your people not working at the Crow during the day?"

Rick asked curiously.

"No, but George will be near," she said.

"Okay."

"What do you suppose I was thinking about?" Jane asked.

Rick didn't answer; he looked at her as she smiled.

"If you must know, it crossed my mind," Jane said.

"There will be other times I hope," Rick said." Although I was instructed not to touch the precious merchandise."

"Yes, Maggie would say something like that, as if I don't have needs," Jane shook her head.

"I'm sure you have needs, and if I can be of any help to your needs, don't be shy! Let me know, and I'll gladly assist you," Rick offered a smile.

"I'm sure you can."

It was eleven forty-five when Rick and Jane got to the "Crow Club," The Matre'd had taken them to a table in the VIP section of the restaurant.

A few minutes later, Mr. Ling Sahig, a potbelly Chinese man in his mid-fifties, joined them at their table.

"Ah, Miss Jane. So nice to see you again," said

Sahig."And, you must be the elusive Rick Drago," he gestured to Rick.

"You have the advantage on me," Rick nodded.

"Allow me to introduce myself. I'm Ling Sahig, the owner of this club, the restaurant you destroyed in London, and the fishing trawler."

"So you're the man responsible for me being here," Rick raised a brow.

Sahig didn't respond; Instead, he claps both hands together, prompting a waiter appeared at the table.

"I hope you don't mind Miss Jane and Mr Rick. I have ordered lunch for all of us," Sahig announced when he spoke to the waiter in Mandarin, and the man disappeared into the kitchen.

After lunch, Rick and Jane followed Sahig to his office, where the discussion about the prototype continued.

"Am I right in thinking you've brought the other section of the prototype with you," Ling asked. "You can speak freely; as the office is soundproof."

"It's here on the island," Rick Drago replied. "You said the other section."

"Yes, I did, didn't I?" Ling sighed. "Not to worry, I don't have it, but I will soon."

"There was another man here on the island

trying to buy the prototype I have, and suddenly I haven't heard from him for quite some time,," Rick Drago stated, while watching for a reaction from Ling.

"What is his name? I like to know the people I'm competing with," Ling Sahig said then crossed his arms.

"He's an American. His name was Frank Allen. Said he was biding for someone in Africa."

This time Rick saw something in Ling's eyes when he looked at his bodyguard, standing close to the office door and beside Rick.

"So you do know him or heard of him?" asked Jane turning in her seat and looking at the bodyguard; Her right hand slid into her purse and gripped her special LCR.38sp.

Jane always felt comfortable with this gun, as it was easy to shoot without taking it out of her purse.

Today Rick was packing an HK.45C his new gun of choice since he got rid of the Magnum. The.45c was now in his hand under the table, aiming at the belly of Ling Sahig.

The bodyguard made a step towards Jane; She fired two shots easily hitting the big Chinese man in the stomach who rushed her, Jane fired again and this time the bullet struck him in the center of his forehead.

Rick was out of his seat and around to the

other side of the table in a flash.

He smashed the butt of his gun across the face of Ling Sahig, rocking him backward in his chair.

Drago's kept his left knee firmly planted in Ling's gut. He jammed the gun in his mouth while Jane guarded the door.

"Who has the other half of the device? And where will you pick it up?" Rick Drago demanded.

Ling shook his head from side to side.

"Tell me!" Rick Drago commanded.

There was no answer from Ling Sahig. This time Drago brought the gun around, striking Ling on his jaw; He knocked teeth out along with a gush of blood.

Rick then attached the silencer before passing the weapon down atop Ling's knee, Rick Drago fired a bullet The Chinese man tried to scream, but Rick's left hand was over his mouth.

"Now, if you don't want to be a cripple, you'll tell me what I want to know," Rick Drago snapped. Ling nod his head in the affirmative.

Rick Drago removed his knee from Ling's stomach and stood up, putting the gun to the temple of Sahig while Ling was trying to stop the bleeding, holding his wounded knee with both hands.

"Write the name, address, and time on a piece of paper!" Rick Drago ordered.

Ling Sahig did as instructed and handed the paper to Drago.

"One more thing," Rick continued. "Who killed Frank Allen?"

Ling pointed to the bodyguard lying on the floor.

"Thank you," Rick said before squeezing the trigger of his gun sending the bullet right through the man's temple.

Jane and Rick left through the back door of the office. Upon exiting, they saw Ling's chauffeur standing by the limousine. With a smile on her face, Jane walked up to him and fired two shots, one bullet hitting the man in his foot, the other bullet hit him in his head.

George was sitting in a Range Rover in the parking lot, seeing Jane and Rick, he got out of the car and approached them. He then gave George the piece of paper with the information from ling Sahig.

"Have your people move on this address and recover that section of the prototype," Rick Drago ordered.

"Are you guys all right," George asked.

"Yeah, we are," Jane replied.

George returned to his Range Rover, shouting into his handheld radio.

"Where too?" Jane asked with a curious look while she and Rick Drago got into her car.

"I'll leave that up to you," Rick Drago shrugged.

"Okay, good. I have to go by my office and check on the team," Jane said as she floored the pedal on the 450SEL Mercedes.

Rick couldn't help but admire her while she navigated the curves in the narrow country road of Haiti at such a high speed.

People were walking by the side of the road on the outskirt of Port-au-Prince carrying baskets on their heads laden with vegetables and fruits.

Others carried massive jugs of water on their shoulders.

Jane slowed the Mercedes as she entered the city limits of Port-au-Prince, Haiti.

"There's always plenty of people along this street all trying to get a travel visa to visit America," Jane stated with sympathy in her voice.

"Can you blame them? This place is in bad shape, economy-wise."

"The families rotate so they won't lose their position in line, dad in line gets relieved by mom then son, the daughter. The bigger the family, the easier and faster for them," Jane explained.

She turned on Route-de-Tabarre, driving at a slow speed, then entered through the gate of the American Embassy. She showed her credentials to the guard in order for them to get in.

Jane parked the car in the space reserved for her. She and Rick Drago then entered the building.

Jane's office occupies part of the third floor in the Embassy; now, she takes the stairs ahead of Drago.

"Have a seat, Rick, " Jane ordered as they entered her office. "I have to file a report on what took place this afternoon."

"Too much damn paperwork each time you go on a job, then some desk jockey scrutinizes your report and finds fault of the way you did your job," he rolled his eyes.

"Yea, that's why I like to make sure that all the T's crossed, before filing my reports," Jane Blackwell said.

Rick Drago got up from his seat and walked around the office; He looked outside through every window while he did.

"What are you looking for?"

"Just checking your escape route from this office in case you can't use the stairs."

"It's in the washroom," she shook her head.

"After you finish your report, what's next?" he questioned.

"Oh, I don't know. Do you have something on your mind?" Jane raised a brow.

"Are you asking me a question like that!" he exclaimed.

"Well! do you?" she pressed.

"Do I what?" Rick Drago teased.

"Have something on your mind?"

He walked over to her desk, tilted her head back, and kissed her on the lips.

"That's what you have on your mind," she breathed.

"What's wrong with that?" Rick Drago asked.

"The timing is terrible. A girl's body has to do what it has to do to keep her healthy," Jane stated.

"It's that time for you, is it?" he asked with discontent.

"Yes, it is," Jane replied.

"It wasn't meant to be," Rick Drago said with a disappointed tone in his voice.

"You could extend your time if you wanted too," she shrugged.

"Wish I could, but duty calls, and I must obey. I can return if you don't mind," he suggested.

"I'll like that; Yeah, I like that very much," Jane smiled.

Rick and Jane's left her office and headed to the hotel and got Rick Drago luggage for his flight back to Bermuda, then to Frank's condo. Rick had a final look around before leaving the island of Haiti; He didn't know what he was hoping to find.

Rick and Jane entered the condo once lived in

by Frank. Boxes of items were laying on the floor with a United States delivery address written on them.

They had cleaned the condo, the furniture neatly in place.

Rick stepped through the front door, leaving Jane inside, while a young boy rode his bike into the front yard of the adjoining building.

"He's never coming back," said the boy to Rick when he noticed him. "My friend is gone."

"He was my friend, too," Rick Drago stated with a frown.

"Mister! Why did he leave without telling me goodbye?" the teary-eyed boy asked.

"He probably left at night and didn't want to wake you from sleeping; I'm sure he didn't do it purposely," he assured the little boy.

"Well. When you see mister Frank, please say I miss him," the boy ride away on his bike.

Jane came out of the condo and joined Rick Drago. Then they got into her car and headed to the airport for Rick's flight back to Bermuda, as the dark clouds covered the sun.

"I think the rain is on its way. It usually rain heavy for a few minutes then it would stop and the sun will come back out again," Jane stated.

She dropped Rick off at the entrance to the departure area. After saying their goodbyes, she drove away with a feeling of despair.

They delayed Rick Drago flight because of the weather condition. He sat in the airport lounge and waited patiently until the flight was ready to leave.

Maggie met Rick on arrival in Bermuda. After a warm welcome, she brought him up to date on what had happened while he was in Haiti.

"You leave for Montreal tomorrow!" Maggie exclaimed with harshness in her voice as she got behind the wheel of her white Rolls Royce.

"We're riding in style today," he observed.

"I thought you'd like it," Maggie said, powering the car out of the parking area.

"Anything from Michael?" he asked.

"Yes, Diana was still in Montreal, and so far, she's only made one trip to Plattsburg, New York." Maggie replied.

"And the General?" he continued.

"David got hit by a van when he crossed the street in front of a hotel. He had a reservation for three people that night, but there's been no word on who the other two people are."

"Is he dead?" he questioned.

"No, he's alive, but according to the information received by the General, he will not be alive much longer, the General wants you to call him ASAP."

Rick Drago used the car phone and called General Applewaite.

"Ah Drago," the General answered the other line. "It's nice to hear from you. I heard you enjoyed the weather in Haiti and willing to go back."

"The weather is gorgeous there," Rick Drago replied.

"You leave for Montreal tomorrow; I'm hoping David is still alive when you get there. He refuses to talk to the police, but maybe he'll talk to you."

"Will you make the arrangements for me to see him!" Rick Drago questioned.

"Don't worry about that. An old friend of yours is handling the case," said the General.

"Think I know who that'll be."

"You'll be met at the airport; Good luck and keep me informed." the General replied.

"Thanks for all your help, General," Rick Drago said before hanging up the phone.

The next day Rick boarded the flight for Montreal. He thought about his friend Jackie as the plane got airborne and wondered if she was still with the Montreal police department and if she ever got married or still single.

Five hours later, the plane touched down at the Pierre Elliot Trudeau airport in Montreal.

The stewardess that served him during the

flight slipped a note in his hand with her name and phone number it read. "Call me?" in red lipstick.

Not having to wait for any luggage as his only piece was the carry-on, Rick headed for the exit just after disembarking.

Chapter Seven

Displaying a sign with Rick Drago written in bold letters was none other than Jackie, who then laid it down to welcome Rick back to Montreal with open arms.

There was no resistance from Rick while Jackie hold his face with both her hands and looked into his eyes.

"I didn't realize how much I've miss you until a few moments ago," Jackie said with a sniffle.

"Miss you too," Rick Drago replied, laying the bag down and putting his arms around Jackie.

"Tony is at the hospital; I'm to take you directly there," Jackie stated.

"And here I thought we had time for a little extra activity," Rick smiled.

"In due time," Jackie offered a small grin in return.

"How bad is David?"

"He's taken a turn for the worst."

"A turn for the worst? As I understand he was already there, anything worst would be dead," he raised a brow.

"Any information on the vehicle that hit him?" Drago questioned.

"The police found the van; Someone set it on fire."

"What about his daughter Diana? Has she visited him?"

"No. I'm not sure will have to check and see if she visited him," Jackie shrugged.

They arrived at the hospital, Tony was there, with Diana pacing up and down in the room. Another older woman sat in the unit's corner.

Her dress was low cut, showing just enough of her chest not to leave anything to the imagination; Rick couldn't help but look, and she caught his eye with a smile. It was obvious she taken care of her body over the years.

"Hi old sock," Lieutenant Tony Bourgaize said, shaking Drago's hand.

"Hi Lieutenant Bourgaize," Drago continued. "Any change in his condition?"

"No change."

Diana saw Rick and walked over to him.

"Thanks for coming," she said.

"I'm here on business, not a social visit," Drago stated.

"Do you know my mother?" Diana asked Drago, looking at the woman sitting in the unit's corner.

"No, I don't," he replied stiffly.

Diana took Rick and introduced him to her mother. "Rick, my mother Dorothy Mercier," she gestured to him with a weak smile. Mom, this is the man that rescued me in London.

Dorothy Mercier remained sitting and outstretched her hand. Rick took it and felt a squeeze that was firm yet inviting.

"Pleasure to meet you, Rick," said Mrs. Mercier.

"The pleasure is all mine," Rick replied.

"He will help solve our problems," Diana announced.

"All of our problems, I hope he can," said Mrs. Mercier in a soft and sultry voice.

"I'll do my best to bring this issue to an end," Rick promised.

An alarm went off as David Mercier went into convulsion. The doctor rushed in and everyone to leave the room.

Minutes later, the doctor came out of the unit leaving a nurse at the bedside and said he would only allow one person at a time to visit David Mercier.

"Are you seeing him? Only one person at a time ordered the doctor," Mrs. Dorothy Mercier questioned.

When the doctor turned away to leave.

"Doctor, this is Rick Drago, he arrived hoping to have a word with my father," said Diana. " He came in from Bermuda."

"You may be too late, Mr.Drago, he's slipping

in and out," the doctor informed him.

It confused Rick Drago how Diana knew he had arrived from Bermuda.

He entered the room and went to the head of the bed.

"Sir, I saw his right hand moved," the nurse beside the bed gasped.

David made a gesture for Rick to come closer. Rick put his ear to David's lips and listened as the dying man ushered the word "boiler." with his last breath.

The doctor entered the unit and checked on David.

Rick then left the room and joined the others waiting outside in the aisle.

"What did he say?" Diana asked, looking at Rick.

"He wanted to say something but couldn't," Rick replied as he stood beside Tony. "Did he say anything when they brought him in?"

"He said nothing to my men," replied Tony. "We interviewed the paramedics, and they say he passed out when they got him into the ambulance."

"David got hit by a vehicle that never stopped, and no one saw anything, not even the make of the car or the license plate numbers," Rick mused. It seemed too good to be true.

"Looks like a planned hit," Tony observed.

"Yes, all the makings of dead men can't talk."

Dorothy Mercier sat with her legs partly open, and her eyes fixed on Rick when he came back into the waiting room.

Rick knew what she was doing, and he let her know he liked it.

She reached into her handbag, and put on a pair of dark glasses, then she got up and walked close to Rick, as she left the waiting area without so much as a teardrop.

Dorothy walked the long corridor until she reached the elevator and waited.

"My mom wants you to follow her. She would like to have a word with you in private," said Diana.

"Your mother will have to wait!" exclaimed Rick "You can tell her I'll see her some other time."

He couldn't believe how much Diana and her mother looked more like sisters than mother and daughter.

Rick sat down with his friend Tony and went over the events leading up to David's demise.

"Boiler. Have you heard this word before?" Rick questioned.

"Boiler?"

"Yes, Boiler, that's the last word from David before he died."

"Never seen it on any information about the

stolen prototype."

"I don't know if it's a password or a code," Rick thought aloud.

"Did you see the expression on Diana's mother's face?" Tony asked. "Almost as if she was happy that the man died."

"Maybe she found out the truth about Mercier and what he did to her family, lying to her about her first husband, Sir Conrad."

"Maybe"

"How much do you know about this prototype that's gone missing?" Rick asked.

"Not much."

"Let's get out of here!" Rick exclaimed.

"Where too?"

"Someplace a little more private."

"Come on; I know just the place," Tony said as they walked out of the hospital and got into the unmarked police cruiser.

Twenty minutes later, Tony pulled into the driveway of his home.

"Here we are," Tony said.

"This is your home," Rick frown, it wasn't what he had in mind.

"What better place; And you didn't get the chance to visit my home the first time you were here," Tony stated.

They got out of the car and walked to the front of the house as Tony's wife opened the front door.

"Here we are," Tony said.

"Rick . This is my wife Carla, Carla. Meet Rick Drago."

"Please to meet you Mr. Rick Drago."

"It's nice to meet you, Mrs. Bourgaize."

Tony took Rick down to the basement, leaving his wife upstairs.

"Two companies built this piece of machinery; One part would be made here in Quebec, and the other in Vancouver. David Mercier was the head of security at the plant here when the piece was stolen," Rick Drago stated.

"How big is this prototype?"

"Each piece can fit into a large suitcase so anyone would have two bags if they had both pieces, and the pieces are not that heavy."

"Canadians developed this machinery?" .

"Yes, two scientists working at a university in Vancouver made the discovery. It extracted salt from seawater for those African countries to have fresh, clean water," Rick stated.

"And the Americans aren't involved in this?" Tony raised a brow.

"Why don't I send you the information I have uncovered. You can read it when you have more time," said Rick. "I must go; There are some important calls I have to make."

"I'll drive you to your hotel!" Tony suggested.

"I have a reservation at The Queen Elizabeth hotel."

The two men left the basement, and Tony kissed his wife before getting into the car to drive Rick to his hotel.

'I think Diana and her mother are staying at the Queen Elizabeth,"

"Don't know what's with Dorothy."

"What do you mean? What's with her?" Tony queried.

"According to Diana, Dorothy wanted to have a private meeting with me when she left the hospital," Rick Drago replied.

"You can have it at the hotel, either in your suite or hers," Tony laughed.

Rick Drago didn't respond as Tony pulled the car into the hotel driveway.

"When are you planning to leave?" asked Tony. "And what about Jackie? Aren't you going to spend time with her?"

"I'll call her," Rick stated before getting out of the car and entering the hotel the car and entering the hotel lobby.

At the front desk, Rick sign the guest book, then took the key-card and went to his suite, while the bell-boy carried the one piece of Rick's luggage.

"What's your name?" Rick asked.

"Andrew."the bell-boy answered.

Rick looked and found information on rental companies. He put an order in to rent a car.

After a short nap, Rick called General Applewaite and informed him about the death of David Mercier.

He then called Jackie.

"Where are you?" asked Jackie after answering the phone.

"I'm at the Queen Elizabeth Hotel. Why don't you come over and have dinner with me?"

"What time should I be there?" she asked.

"Whenever you're ready, I'll be here," Rick promised.

Jackie arrived at the hotel at six-thirty in the evening.

"Do you want to go down to the restaurant or have room service?" Rick asked.

"Room service is a great idea," Jackie suggested.

After supper, Rick and Jackie talked about the first day they meet and what Joanne was doing, and his visit to Barbados.

Rick put a stop to her questions, taking her in his arms and began kissing her.

Jackie stayed with Rick until the next morning.

She left the hotel at seven the next morning, went home, took a shower and a change of clothes, then headed to the police headquarters.

After Jackie left the suite, Rick called Michael in London, England.

"Hello mate," said Michael answering his cell phone.

"Hello yourself, Mike," Rick replied.

"Bad news about David Mercier."

"Yes, I'm staying at the same hotel as Diana and her mother, Dorothy."

"Did you had a chat with either of them?"

"About one minute with Dorothy she's not a bad-looking woman."

"Don't tell me you're thinking of making a move on her?" queried Michael.

"No, not me," Rick laugh.

"What's your next move?"

"To put an end to this and go visit a few friends in Barbados," Rick replied.

"I'm going to Barbados in July, got an invitation from an old friend to come and see the carnival there," Michael informed him..

"I'll keep you up to date from this end," Rick promise before turning off the phone.

The phone in Rick's hotel suite rang.

"Hello," he greeted as he picked up the receiver.

"This is the front desk. Your rental car is here, and you need to sign the rental agreement papers,

Mr. Drago. should I sent her up to your suite, or will you be coming down to the lobby?"

"Send the person up!" replied Rick.

After signing the rental contract, Rick took a shower and got dressed.

He then called Tony and explained to him he'd be out and about checking on important information that General Applewaite asked him to look into here in Montreal.

Rick left his suite and took the elevator to the hotel lobby. Down stairs a young couple sat at a coffee table with a view of Rene-Levesque Blvd.

A man sat alone at another table, having a cup of something, and another sat close to the main entrance reading a newspaper.

Rick got into the rental car and drove away from the hotel. He went north along Cote-des-Neiges Blvd, heading for the "mountain" as it was known locally at the top of Mount Royal.

Many people visited the area at night, which was when they could see a display of lights in the city of Montreal.

Rick regularly checks the rear-view mirror and noticed a car behind him and maintaining the same distance.

He increased his speed, going up the hill leading to Mount Royal. Rick remembered there was a sharp drop at the top with parking pace on the left and right side of the road.

Rick park on the left, as there wouldn't as much traffic on the road when he crossed over. He parked with no problem.

The car following Rick had also increased its speed. As it reaches, the top the driver didn't see Rick's car ahead of him anymore. He was looking for Rick and wasn't paying attention to where he was driving, when suddenly a street sweeper vehicle was in front of him.

The driver suddenly turned the wheel to avoid hitting the sweeper and ran into the guardrail. The vehicle flipped over and crashed down the side of the mountain before bursting into flames.

Other vehicles slowed down, looking at the crashed car. Some of them parked while other kept ongoing.

Rick got out of his car and walked to the place where the vehicle crashed through the rail; he was looking at the burning car when he heard a voice.

"Good evening Mr. Rick Drago, I warned him not to take you alone, but he didn't listen," said the man as he put a gun in Rick's back.

Rick then tried to turn and face the man talking.

"Oh no, Mr. Rick. Walk ahead of me!" His adversary ordered. "To the car in front of yours."

Reaching the car, Rick reached for the door handle.

"No, Rick! Let me help you," said the man as he walks around to face Rick.

The man was one of the two men Rick had seen in the lobby back at the hotel.

He kept the gun pointed at Rick and opened the car door with his other hand. As the door swung out, Rick swiftly push the door wider, hitting the man and knocking him off balance.

Rick then slides across the back of the car, putting the vehicle between himself and the man. He drew his weapon and fired a shot, hitting the man right in the ankle.

The man fired shots into the air as he tumbled to the ground. He then tried to put his gun in play, but before he did, Rick was there to step on the hand holding the weapon. He crushed the wrist into the ground.

Rick took the weapon from the man and tossed it over the side of the mountain while the man screamed obscenities at him.

"I need information, and you will give it to me," Rick grinned.

"You bastard. You'll get nothing from me," the man snapped.

"You can save yourself a lot of pain if you just talk to me," said Rick. He then heard sirens and knew the police and fire trucks would soon be there.

Rick opened the trunk of the car and ordered the man to get in, with a convincing kick on the damaged ankle.

Then Rick drove the car to the underground parking area of the Cote-des-Neiges shopping mall.

Rick found a space and parked the car. Then he used the remote control and opened the trunk.

The man in the trunk had never moved.

"You've lost a lot of blood and if you don't get medical attention for your ankle, you could bleed to death," Rick chuckled.

"Help me out of here!" the man pleaded.

"Not before you give me some answers," Rick shrugged.

"Everything was done by phone they hired us to monitor two women staying at the hotel, then we got another call to look out for a man fitting your description."

"Go on!" Rick commanded. "But first, tell me about David Mercier."

"We were keeping tabs on Mercier. He got suspicious and tried to outsmart us by parking his car, then he took a taxi, got out a few blocks away and went through alley got back in his car and drove away."

"What happened after?" Rick asked.

"Mercier tried to do the same thing again, and something went wrong," said the man.

"Something went wrong all right, David was a rat, but we allow even rats to live, and I'm not fond of people trying to kill me," Rick muttered.

"We got orders not to harm the women, but if the opportunity arose, we should get rid of you," the man said. "Now, will you help me out of here?"

"One more thing. This person on the phone. Did he have an accent? What accent did he have?"

"He sounded like Chinese or Japanese, you know from one of those countries," explained the man. "I told you all I know. If you're going to kill me, get it over with, I'd rather you do it than to stay here and bleed to death."

"Give me your cell phone!" Rick commanded.

"Why?"

"Because you won't be needing it anymore," said Rick as he shot the man in his forehead and closed the trunk.

In all fairness, Rick often wondered how enthusiastic he would be about carrying out his assignments if he, like most of his counterparts, had to worry about his actions being the gossip of white-collar discussion or making headline news.

Rick took a taxi back to his car, Firetrucks, ambulance, and police officers were all at the scene of the burnt-out vehicle when he arrived.

He got into his car, put a call through to Tony.

"Hello Rick. Where are you?"

"On the mountain. They followed me from the hotel by two cars, one driver flipped over the guard rail when he lost control, and the car burst into flames, the fire trucks and police are here now."

"Have they questioned you?"

"No. There's something else. The driver of the other car can be found in the trunk of his car in the underground parking area of the shopping mall."

"Is he?"

"Yes he is," Rick responded, then he turned off the phone and drove away.

It was late in the evening when Rick drove along Park Avenue, heading north away from the city of Montreal. About 30 meters back, Rick noticed a vehicle trying to maintain the distance behind his car.

As the traffic thinned out the driver decided to closed the distance, Rick increased the speed crossing over the highway and into the working district with massive warehouses, then he turned between two huge buildings and stopped the car.

Rick got out of the vehicle, crossing over to the other side. He then walked back a few paces to the main door of a building. He went up to the steps and stood with his back to the wall while the vehicle following him drove past at a slow speed; it stopped a few meters on the other side of the street where Rick had his car parked.

The driver of the car remained seated behind the wheel while lighting a cigarette and lowering the window. Rick was there, and the driver felt the cold nozzle of this gun against the side of his neck.

"Both hands on the wheel!" commanded Rick.

The driver did as was ordered.

"Why are you following me?"

"No need for the gun, I'm just following you to see where you go and who you meet," replied the driver.

Rick opened the car door before stepping away.

"Get out, turn around, and spread your feet apart!" he ordered.

The driver did as instructed. Rick patted him down and found a weapon, a wallet containing a driver's license, and a few other identification papers.

"You will not tell me anything, are you?" Rick asked.

"You know I will not give you any

information," replied the man.

"I didn't think so, Zhen," said Rick before redialing Tony's number.

"Who are you calling," asked Zhen.

"A babysitter to keep watch over you."

"Is she good-looking?" Zhen laughed.

"Yes, she's good-looking and just as dangerous. You'll enjoy every minute with her," Rick assured him.

The lights of two vehicles approached fast, Rick took hold of Zhen's shirt and forced him onto his knees while holding the gun to his head.

"If they're friends of yours, the first thing that's going to happen is, you'll get a bullet to the back of your skull, and then I'll deal with them," Rick said in his ear.

As the cars approached, Rick realized it was Jackie followed by another unmarked police car.

"What gives?" Jackie asked when she got out of the car after parking it. "Tony said you needed my help right away."

"Yes, I need your help," said Rick. "I have to check on something for the General. First, two guys followed me who are now dead, then this other guy shows up. Will you run a check on him and keep him on ice for me?"

"For you? You know I will," Jackie smiled.

"Good. I'll do this thing for the General and meet you at headquarters later."

Jackie nodded to the other detective, who then put the cuffs on Zehn. He put the man in the back of his police car.

Rick got into his car and drove away.

"Who's that guy?" the detective asked. "I've seen him before."

"He's a special agent out of the USA. He was here a little while ago, working on another case. You might have seen him then," Jackie replied.

"Yeah, I know, but who is he, really?"

"Do you think you've lived long enough?" Jackie sighed.

"No. Why do you ask?"

"Because if you ask too many questions about him, he has a license to kill," she said .

"You mean like James Bond? That kinda license?"

"Exactly," Jackie continued. "So no more questions."

"The two of you seem very close," he observed.

"Yes, we're good friends."

"Looks like more than just friends to me," he raised a brow.

"You think!" said Jackie with a roll of her eyes. "Let's go."

Rick arrived at the address in the north-end of Montreal, where he's to receive information for General Applewaite.

He went up the front steps of the house and press the doorbell.

"Who is it?" a woman's voice asked before opening the door.

"I'm here on behalf of General Applewaite."

"One moment please." the woman said.

Rick heard the chain being removed from the door, then it opened a middle age looking woman was standing with a sealed large envelope in her hands.

"You must be Mr. Rick?" she stated.

"Yes I am," he replied.

"I was expecting you earlier," she said with a frown.

"Traffic."

She handed the large envelope to Rick.

He took the envelope. "The General appreciate this very much," while turning and heading back to his vehicle.

Rick opened the envelope and examined its contents before driving off.

It said the items were at a wear-house outside the city of Toronto.

Rick then called the police headquarters and spoke with Tony.

"I have to travel to Toronto, I'll try to book on the next flight from Dorval airport," he said.

"We ran your friend's fingerprints through our computer, and Interpol wants him. He's been a bad boy doing bad things for anyone if the price is right," Tony retorted.

"What about Diana and her mother, Dorothy?" asked Rick.

"They took a flight to Toronto earlier this afternoon."

"Okay. I'll check in with Michael back in London. He has a man keeping tabs on them," Rick replied.

"Okay," said Tony. "You want to talk with Jackie?"

"I'll call her after I reach Toronto."

Rick went back to the hotel and checked out. He then arranged with the rental company to drop the rental car off at Dorval airport.

Rick got his ticket and boarded the flight to Toronto international airport.

Chapter Eight

Waiting at the Toronto airport for Rick was a tall, broad-shouldered man holding a placard with his name written on it.

"Hi, I'm Sam Harris, The General sends his

regards," said the man with an outstretched hand.

Rick shook the man's hand, after feeling his firm grip Drago applied a little pressure of his own; both men looked at each other with a smile.

"Please to meet you," Rick said.

"Same here. The General holds you in high regards," Sam stated. They walked out of the airport and into the parking area where Sam had parked his car.

The two men got into the car. " Here is the address   where we have to go," Rick said handing a note to Sam.

"We'll take the Don Valley express," Sam said.

"I'll leave the driving to you."

The traffic on the Don Valley express was moving much slower than usual.

"The Maple Leaf hockey team is playing at home. That's the reason the traffic is moving this slow," Sam said.

"Are they any good? I mean the hockey team," queried Rick.

"No, they aren't good, but the fans love them. They sell the stadium out for every home game," Sam shook his head. "We'll get off at the next exit."

The building Rick was looking for displayed its name in large brass letters and numbers. Standing at the gate was two armed guards checking the cars before waving them through.

"Looks like some fancy shin-ding is going on here at the moment," said Sam. "What now?"

"We go in!" Rick exclaimed. "Those guards don't know who to turn away; they're only there to scare away the bad guys."

"What are we? The good guys?" Sam queried .

"We know who we are, but the guards don't know."

A Mercedes tried to go past the Audi, but Sam would have no part of jogging for a position with the Benz to go past the guards at the gate.

A guard saw what happened and came over to the cars.

"What seems to be the problem here?" he asked.

"I'm here waiting for my turn to enter. The person in the Mercedes seems to be in a hurry and tried to get ahead of me," Sam replied.

The guard walked to the Benz and asked the driver to back up the car, allowing Sam to go through.

The valet attendant was waiting for Sam to stop so he could park the Audi, but Sam continued to drive and found a place at the back of the building.

They were many reasons Sam didn't allow anyone to park the Audi. The entire car was bulletproofed and carried many weapons inside the vehicle and in the trunk.

Rick got into the back seat of the car. From his carry-on bag, he took out a suit of clothing and slid into them.

Sam did the same after retrieving his own clothing from the trunk of the car, along with hardware for both himself and Rick.

They walked back to the front of the building, but before entering, Sam got a dirty look from the valet was in line to park his car, causing Sam to dig into his wallet.

"Got change from a twenty?" Sam asked, handing the money to the valet.

"Sure," replied the young man, his hand came out of his pocket with nothing. "So sorry sir, I gave all my small bills away making change."

"That's okay," Rick said patting the valet on his shoulder "monitor the Audi and keep the twenty!"

"Gee, mister. Thanks," the young man said. "Where did you park?"

"At the back of the building."

"Not to worry, I'll find it," the valet promised.

No one was at the entrance leading into the building. Everyone entered and seemed to wait for the host to appear. The aroma of expensive cologne, along with cigars, filled the room.

Sam thought they might have stuck out like a sore thumb. Upon entering, the first person he saw was a beautiful black woman sitting alone.

Rick watched as Sam made his move towards the lady.

Rick then mingled with the crowd, taking a glass of champagne from a tray as a waiter passed.

Rick checked for exits from the room and thought the cameras were recording the people when they entered to check their identities.

Sam Harris was now engaged in conversation with three women when two other women joined the black woman.

Rick looked at his watch; the timepiece said eight fifty in the evening, which meant in ten minutes the host of the party should have appear.

Rick could sense the wealth of the people. Arabs, Egyptian, Africans, Chinese, Japanese, and South American all waiting for the host to appear.

Rick estimated there were three women to each man. Rick can't remember the last time he saw so many beautiful women in the same place and time.

A large clock on the wall rang out, and the room became silent. Suddenly, the sound of instrumental music filled the air as the clock struck nine o'clock.

Two men appeared each one wearing a white suit that looked a little too small for their bulky figure, as they descended the stairwell followed by two Japanese men wearing loose-fitting clothes made of multicolor silk cloth, one of them wore a red Fez hat on his head the other man seemed to go bald, and three other men dressed in dark suits followed.

From the look of their faces, they look like twins.

Rick and the bald-headed man locked eyes. Rick et his glass down on a nearby table and made his way through the crowd.

Rick remembered the face after seeing him leaving the hotel in Montreal and getting into a Limousine when he was checking in.

He also remembered the description he got from the General contact in Montreal.

The crowd had now created a human wall some men was holding envelopes in their hands while the two bodyguards dressed in white moved through the crowd to collect them.

The bald-headed man address the guests when they reached the last landing of the stairs.

"Good evening, everyone. My name is Lucas Connors, and I'm your host for this evening. And this is the Hijiri." he gestured to the other Japanese man standing beside him.

Standing over six feet tall, Rick looked over to where Sam Harris had been talking to those women earlier, but he wasn't there.

Sam Harris was standing at arm's length from

Lucas Connors and the Hijiri. The two men dressed in white had finished their duties collecting the items from the guests.

Rick moved closer to where his friend was standing.

Lucas said something to the Hijiri and turned to walk away, then stopped. Sam Harris moved from his position to get closer to Lucas and the Hijiri.

The crowd had got bigger and was now surrounding the Hijiri and Lucas. The dark-suited bodyguards made their way through the crowd and cleared a path for Lucas and the Hijiri.

Sam held his position as Rick went behind the Hijiri, Lucas and the three bodyguards.

Sam sees two oriental men appear on the stairs at the back of Rick. Sam Harris nodded to Rick. He turned his head and saw the men, each one has a sword on his side, and a dagger stuck in the waist-band.

Sam walked back and joined Rick. The men came down the stairs, then turned and walked away from the crowd, Rick and Sam followed them. While the other guests walked through the hallways and into the area specially prepared for the evenings event.

Rick Drago and Sam Harris enter the room behind the men.

The door behind them slammed shut. Looking around, they saw there was no other exit, Sam Harris and Rick was cut off from the other guest.

A glass panel opened, and the two men with swords stepped into the room. Sam Harris went into action and with outstretched arms Sam tackled them to the ground.

Rick moved in and took one of them by the hand, twisting it with such speed and force that he snapped the man's wrist. Rick then took a dagger and cut across the man's throat.

Sam Harris right fist smashed against the other man's temple and blood gushed from under the man's head onto the floor.

Rick Drago and Sam Harris left the room through the same opening where the men entered and came face to face with a huge Japanese man.

Rick was in no mood for a fist to fist showdown he drew his gun and fired the bullet shattered the man's knee. He went to the floor in a heap.

"Where are they?" Drago asked, stepping on the shattered knee.

There was no answer. The man drew a dagger from his waistband and tried to swing it at Rick Drago's leg, just as Sam's right foot came down on his wrist, crushing it against the tiled floor.

"Where are they?" Rick repeated his question.

With his right hand, the man pointed to the stair-well, which had two landings. Rick shot him in his forehead without hesitation.

Sam Harris and Rick Drago headed up the stairs to reach the first of the two landings. They saw a young man standing in front of a door. As Rick and Sam got closer to the entrance, the man took a blade from the waistband in his back.

Rick shot the young man in the chest, and the man fell to one knee. An older man opened the door, stepped out of the room and charge at Sam swinging a sword while he backed away.

Rick now focused on the swordsman and Sam, not wanting to fire a bullet. He took a throwing star and skillfully let it fly, finding its mark high in the warrior's shoulder. This caused the sword to drop from his grip.

Sam Harris ducked under the older man's attempted swing at his head and knocked the man to the floor with a kick to the groin.

Seeing Sam was now in control of the situation, Rick stepped over the young man's corpse and entered the room.

Taking no chances with the old warrior, Sam connected with a powerful kick to the warrior's head, and blood squirted from the man's mouth.

Rick searched the room then his friend entered and joined him.

"Look at this!" Sam said.

"What is it?" Rick asked without looking at him.

"It's an envelope like the ones that was collected earlier from the guests," Sam replied.

Rick took the envelope from Sam and opened it. Inside was a name and numbers with a dollar sign.

"They were bidding on something," Sam observed.

"Yes, and that something, was the prototype," replied Rick.

Meanwhile, they continued to search the room.

A white-suited man entered the room, Rick back was to the door, the man hold him from behind trying to put Rick in a bear hug, Rick lowered his body while he held the man by his hand, pulling him forward and over his right shoulder.

Sam Harris threw two mighty fists into the fallen man's stomach. The big man's eyes opened wider while Rick applied pressure to his elbow.

"Where are they? Rick demanded."And. what's your name?"

"Lucas Connors left. The Hijiri is still here, " he replied." And my name's Yuto Ogawa, my brother name is Yuki Ogawa.

"Where did Lucas Connors go?" Rick tighten his grip on Yuto's elbow.

"I don't know." he answered annoyingly.

"Does Lucas Connors live here?" .

"No. This is the Hijiri's home, Lucas Connors is the Hijiri secretary."

"How long has he worked for the Hijiri?" Rick questioned with a drawled.

"About six months." he answered painfully.

"One last question," Rick said." Who do you work for?"

"My brother and I work for the Hijiri, we're a part of his security team."

"Why did the other guards interfere when we tried to get to Lucas Connors?"

"They thought you were here for the Hijiri," he infuriatingly replied.

"You said security at this residence. There's another home own by the Hijiri?" Rick inquired.

"He has another home in the city of Toronto, but I've never been there."

Rick and Sam then helped the man from the floor and into a chair.

"You will explain to the Hijiri that our presence here has nothing to do with him. We were here for Lucas Connors, who's an evil man."

Sam chimed in. "And on behalf of the Government of Ontario accept our apologies."

Rick and Sam left the room and took the stairs, once they reached the top of the second landing, Rick signaled for Sam to check the rooms on the left, while he checked the ones on the right.

In a crouched position, Rick opened the first door and looked inside. It was the security room equipped with TV monitors; he saw that reel tapes were still recording.

Rick looked at a live feed from a camera showing the front of the house. One of the car valets was helping another valet from the ground.

Rick zoomed in on the young men, then on the driveway leading to the gate. He then saw the red lights of a car leaving as Sam entered the room.

"Those rooms are empty," he said.

"A car just went through the main gate, let's hope it's Lucas Connors," Rick said when he stopped the machine and removed the reel tape.

"We can catch him if we get out of here," suggested .

"We go now!" Rick ordered.

Reaching outside, Sam saw the attendant he'd told to watch his car bending over in pain.

"What happen to you?" he asked the valet.

"I brought Mr. Connors's car around, and he pulled me from behind the wheel and threw me onto the ground, hurting my wrist and ankle then he drove away," the young man explained.

"Was he carrying anything?" asked Rick .

"Yes," said the valet. "He has a case."

"Anyone with him?"

"No. He is alone."

"You should have your injuries checked the sooner the better," Sam advised.

They headed to the back of the building and got into the Audi and drove off.

Rick and his partner had their guns ready when they approached the gate.

The guard at the gate waved them on through, but Sam stopped the Audi before going through the gate.

"Which direction did Lucas Connors go?" Sam asked the guard.

"He went that way," said the guard, pointing toward Toronto.

"Thank you," Sam nodded before driving off, he headed in the same direction, hoping to catch Lucas Connors.

"The Hijiri was still back there in the house," he told Rick.

"He didn't leave the house with Lucas Connors," Rick replied.

"That's why we didn't see the other half of the tag-team brothers. He's guarding the Hijiri," Sam suggested.

"Yes, I think you're right."

"We've been driving for over fifteen minutes, and there's no sign of a silver Benz, I'm afraid he's given us the slip," Sam sighed

"Let's head to the city of Toronto!" Rick

suggested.

"We'll have the airport watched," Sam said as he got on the car phone and made a call to the General.

"Hello Sam," General Applewaite said when he answered the phone.

"Connors gave us the slip at the home of the Hijiri, and according to the guard at the gate, he was heading toward Toronto. We followed but didn't catch up to him," Sam explained.

"Where are you now?"

"On our way to Toronto."

"Okay," the General said, then he hung up.

"Where are you booked for your stay in Toronto?" Sam asked his friend.

"The Holiday Inn," Rick replied.

"After you've settled in, why don't you come with me to a all night party," Sam offered.

"I have to make a few calls," Rick shrugged.

"I Will pick you up in an hour!" he said.

Ninety minutes later, Sam and Rick entered the home of Marcus Penosa.

Women dressed in suits. Others wore evening gowns with openings up to the hips, and some wore low cut front and back cut-out dresses.

"Who's the host?" Rick asked Sam.

"His name is Marcus Penosa, and he's into the textiles business," his friend replied. " He's also, a travel agent."

"His business seems to do very good," Rick observed.

"The Textiles are a front for what he's really into."

They went to the bar, Sam ordered a Johnnie Walker Black, and Rick ordered a Jack Daniels.

"I'm sorry," said the bartender. "I don't have any Jack Daniels."

"I'll have a Rye on ice," Rick shrugged.

The barman served Rick a shot of twelve-year-old Canadian Club.

"Shall we meet the host?" Sam proposed.

"By all means, lead on," he replied.

They made their way through the crowded dance area until they reached a large oak door.

Sam opened the door and entered with Rick one step behind.

Inside was a lavish room, equipped with a bar, a circle sofa, and on the couch, a man lying with two women naked aside from their slender thongs. They were kissing him fervently.

Two men sat at the bar with their backs to the door and the action on the couch. They now got to their feet when Sam and Rick entered the room.

They covered the floor with thick oriental rugs, and many paintings hung on the walls. There was a large monitor displaying the waves of the ocean rolling onto the beach.

The ceiling, however, was covered with mirrors.

"By whose authority do you enter this room?" asked the man on the couch when he sat up between the two women. He placed his glasses on his face.

"My own Marcus," said Sam "And call off your two goons if you don't want a mess in here."

Marcus Penosa signaled his two men to stand down.

"Who's this you brought with you, Sam?" Marcus Penosa asked.

"You don't want to know. It won't be good for your health," replied Sam.

"What can I do for Toronto's top law enforcer?" he questioned holding the two girls beside him..

"My friend will ask you some questions, and you better provide the right answers. If not, you'll find out why you shouldn't know him," Sam stated.

Marcus Penosa got up from the couch and walked into another room while Rick followed him.

Only then did Rick realize it was the washroom. One chair occupied the room and

Rick motion for Marcus to take a seat.

"I need you to be like a computer. I'll ask the questions, and you will provide me with the right answers!" he ordered.

"If I can," Marcus rolled his eyes.

"You entered this room a proud man, and it's up to you to remain that way," said Rick "Do you know Lucas Connors?"

"Yeah, I know him."

"Do you know about any arrangement he's making to ship an important item out of the country?" Rick demanded.

"they recommended him to me by a mutual friend about a year ago. Since that time, I've brought in rugs and painting for him and the Hijiri." Marcus shrugged.

"I want to know about shipping!" Rick informed him and got infuriated.

"About three weeks ago, he asked about shipping something special, he didn't say what it was," Marcus Penosa shrugged. "I tried to explain to him, that I must know the contents of the item to put it on the shipping manifest, but he didn't give me any details."

"You're also a travel agent. Have you recently made travel arrangements for Lucas Connors and the Hijiri?" Rick asked.

"Yes, this was the second time I'm booking their travels itinerary," Marcus rolled his eyes.

"What date was their flight, and where are they going?"

"The flight's booked for Monday, and they're going to Europe," Marcus replied.

"Where in Europe?" Rick asked vigorously. "Europe's a large continent."

From one pocket of his house robe, Marcus took out an iPhone and punched in some numbers.

"Here it is. The first stop in Sweden, then France, England and then to Japan," he said handing Rick the phone.

"That's an unusual route," Rick replied, raising a brow and handing the phone back to Marcus.

"I'm not sure. I think it's the speaking engagements of the Hijiri," Marcus stated.

"I see a female name on the itinerary, Elizabeth Carson. Do you know her?" Rick asked.

"No. This was the first time I've heard or seen her name," Marcus Penosa continued. "Is that it? I want to get back to those two young animals were about to devour me when you guys barged in."

"No. When was the last time you spoke with Lucas Connors?" Rick snapped.

"He was here earlier tonight. He brought the money for the tickets and picked them up, then he left a few minutes before you guys arrived."

"Did he say where he was going?" Rick asked.

"He said something about returning a car, then he then left with his woman," said Marcus.

"His woman?" Rick asked.

"Yes, she was here," replied Marcus Penosa.

"Now Marcus, you've been good so far. Don't spoil it now. What's her address?" Rick asked.

"I don't know her address, but I know her name, and where she works. Her name is Eva, and she's working tonight at a club downtown name The Miramar," Marcus said.

"You've been very helpful, Marcus, I trust you won't mention this to anyone," Rick patted his shoulder. " Maybe someday I'll repay you."

"I still don't know who you are. You're not from these parts, that much I know," Marcus said.

"As Sam told you, it's best for you not to know," Rick said.

"How about repaying me right now? Sam knows who to talk too about easing off my business," Marcus said.

"I'll talk with Sam about it," Rick promised.

They left the washroom and rejoined the others. The two young women were still lying on the couch, while the bodyguards stood at the entrance to the room.

Rick and Sam left the party and headed downtown Toronto for the Miramar Club.

"Have you visited this club before?" Rick asked Sam.

"Once, last year after the Toronto's Grand Prix race," Sam replied "I know one doorman."

At the door to the Club. Sam chatted with one doorman, then Sam, and Rick entered the Club.

They ushered them to a table near the stage where a young woman was doing a pole dance.

A long-legged waitress came to the table and took the drink orders from the both of them..

Moments later, she returned and set the drinks down on the table.

"When does Eva dance?" Sam asked.

"She starts in about five minutes," replied the waitress.

The lights dimmed, and the music got louder while the MC made his announcement.

"Let's give a warm welcome to our star of the Miramar Club, Madam Eva."

Eva did her dance routine, ending with a blanket spread on the stage as she gyrated, moving her body in various positions, then moving among the tables below the stage.

Reaching their table, Eva sat to the side of Sam.

Rick then raised his hand and to get the attention of the waitress.

"What are you going to have?" he asked.

"She knows what to bring me," Eva replied.

"Not the kool-aid! I want to buy you a real drink."

"In that case, we should leave," Eva said. "I'll change."

Moments later, Eva returned. "Shall we go?" she asked.

They got up from their seat, Eva tucked her left hand under Sam's arm and her right under Rick's arm while they walked out of the Club.

"Where are we going?" Sam asked in a curious voice.

"To my place," Eva replied obviously.

"I'll follow you in my car," he said.

"Okay. He stays with me," she said, referring to Rick.

Chapter Nine

Sam then walked to his car, got in, and waited for Eva to drive off.

Ten minutes later, they arrived at Eva's Condominium, as Eva and Rick Drago got out of her car.

"I thought you wanted to be alone with me," Eva pouted.

"Yes, I'll like to be alone with you but not at your place, " Rick said. "I'll rather be alone with you at my hotel suite."

Eva took a key from her purse and unlocked a door revealing a lift, Rick and Eva enter the elevator and waited for Sam.

Her Condominium was on the fifth and last floor, only two Condos on this floor, the other levels have four on each.

"This is home," said Eva while she opened the door to her Condominium.

Rick and Sam follow Eva into her home, she goes behind the bar.

"What will you two gents like to drink?" Eva asked.

"Jack Daniels for me if you have it," Rick said.

"I'll have a scotch on ice," Sam replied.

"Now, when two fine gentlemen offer to buy a nightclub dancer a real drink, there's more to it than a drink. So, what can I do for you?" Eva asked as her house phone rang.

Eva continued to serve Sam and Rick their drinks.

"Why don't you answer your phone?" Sam Harris asked. "It may be important."

"I know who's calling," replied Eva. "And it's not important."

"Your boyfriend's not important?" Rick asked.

"You know him?" Eva queried.

"What's his name?" asked Rick.

"Lucas Connors. And thinks he owns me," Eva said. "He wants to take me to Japan and live with him."

"When was he going to Japan?" Sam asked curiously.

"Yes, he leaves tomorrow morning with the Hijiri, who was going on a European and

Oriental holy tour," Eva said.

"Will he come and visit you before he leaves?" Rick asked.

"No, he's at the home of the Hijiri," replied Eva.

"Thank you, we have to leave, busy day ahead of us," said Sam .

"Lucas Connors told me someone was after him, that won't be you, would it?" queried Eva looking at Rick .

Sam and Rick left Eva's Condo.

"Will, I ever see you again?" Eva asked Rick. "It's over! Lucas Connors and I. Please call me!"

"I'll call you later," said Rick, taking the card from Eva's hand.

"What now?" asked Sam, getting behind the wheel of his car.

"Take me back to the hotel!" said Rick .

"What about Lucas Connors?" asked Sam.

"If Lucas Connors doesn't have the missing piece of the prototype, he knows where it was, and those people invited to see the Hijiri made bids by seal envelopes on something, and I think it's the missing piece. I have to be there when he put his hands on it," Rick said.

"I agree. What do you think about Eva?" asked Sam.

"I'll call her later," Rick said.

"I'll inform the General on what happened

tonight," Sam said.

"Okay. See what you can find out about the woman traveling with the Hijiri; her name is Elizabeth Carson," Rick ordered.

Rick took a shower, then called Eva.

"What took you so long?" Eva said harshly.

"I just came out of the shower and called you before going to bed."

"I'm coming to your hotel, give me the suite number!" Eva commanded.

Minutes later, Eva entered Rick's suite. She left his suite five o'clock the next morning knowing Rick have an early flight.

The next day, Rick boarded the plane. He arrived in Brussels. After checking into the hotel, he went to the Cafe on Paardenmarkt Street at the request of General Applewaite.

The place set back on the corner of a four-way cobblestone intersection, with clothing boutiques, and stores selling furniture, pottery, kitchen items. Rick sat down at a table with a view of the reserved table and the streets. He ignored the reserved table the General said would wait for him.

Rick ordered the Cafe's famous smoked meat sandwich and ate.

Looking over the place at all the young faces.

Rick thought he picked up the voice of an American somewhere down in the corner on his far right.

The General said he was to sit at the reserved table and order something to eat, and then would be contacted.

Rick could see the traffic lights in the square, then he saw a policewoman stopped the traffic, and helped an older man dressed in a wrinkle old grey suit to cross the streets.

The man with a black boulder on his head, slightly bent forward, and shoulders slumped. In one hand an old beat-up umbrella, the other hand in his pocket.

The old gentleman entered the Cafe. It didn't take the Fixer long to recognize the man as Lo Wong. It also didn't surprise Rick that Lo Wong was still among the living.

Lo Wong made his way between the tables and sautered to where Rick was sitting without looking at the reserved table, almost like he knew Drago wouldn't sit at the table in the center of the Cafe.

"Glad you could make it," said Wong as he sat down in a chair where he too could see the entrance into the Cafe.

"Why the meeting?" Rick asked curiously.

"You don't seem surprised to see me," Lo Wong said.

Rick didn't reply to the question from Wong.

"First, I must tell you,. I'm not the enemy," Wong stated, reaching into his jacket pocket.

He didn't see Rick's hand moved, Wong only felt the cold piece of steel pressed against his leg.

"I'm reaching for my ID," said Wong, while he inserted two fingers into the pocket and fished out his ID.

"Slowly!" Rick commanded.

"How perceptive of you, Mr. Drago, I know you're dying to hear what I have to say."

"Well, I'm curious about your motives. Yes, I want to hear what you have to say."

Lo Wong slides a tiny leather folder across the table to Rick. "Open it! Mr. Drago, it will explain certain things before we begin."

The small folder has an ID card and a photo of LO Wong identifying him to be Lieutenant Ly Ling, head of the Hong Kong fraud squad, and a member of Interpol.

"I must get this verified, you understand," Rick said with sarcasm.

Rick calls the General with the information Ly Ling gave to him and listened while the General explains about the Japanese lawman.

After the conference with the General, Rick put away his phone and listened while Ly Ling fill him in on the reason he went undercover and the fanatic group known as C.M.L.F.

"It all started a few years ago when the man you know as Lucas Connors, but, known to me by Kim Ching, defrauded a bank in Hong Kong out of five million American dollars."

Rick listened as the Japanese agent continue. "Kim Ching went free because they killed the two people who could identify him a few days after the crime," Ling continued. "Ching then employed the world most feared swordsmen, and a couple of years ago, he turned up in Japan with the Hijiri."

"The head of the bank which Connors defrauded. Is it your father?"

"Yes. I don't want you to think my family could be so easily tricked," replied Ly as he explains to Rick.

"What do you want from me?" Rick asked. "My leave from the command of the unit ends in two weeks; if I don't capture him by then, I'll be shamed among my colleagues and forced into retirement."

"Why not stay with Interpol until this mess is over?" Rick inquired.

"Papers were signed and agreements made at the highest level in the department, so I have to return."

"Come on! We go," Rick said when he stood up and put a twenty-dollar bill in America currency under the plate.

Ling and Rick had only taken two steps when a waiter carrying a tray with sandwiches dropped it and opened fire at them with an Uzi.

Rick and Ling had seen the movement of the man before the gun went into play.

The "Fixer" Rick hit the floor, turning the table for shelter. Then he took Nellie in his right hand and fired.

Ly Ling opened the old-looking umbrella he was carrying. Crouching behind the Gamp while it protected him from the hail of bullets.

What seemed like second after the shooting started, it ended. The big yank stood up where the gunman had fallen and give Rick the thumbs-up sign.

Rick and Ly walk over to have a closer look at the shooter, under the rib-cage on the left side and a pool of blood.

Rick turned the body over. A bullet had hit the shooter in the chest and another one in the neck. "Do you know him?" he asked.

"No," said Ly Ling. "Mr. Rick, I want you to know, I couldn't allow my cover to be exposed when we first met. I also want you to know that I admire your work a great deal."

Rick looked around to have a word with the big American, but he was gone.

The patrons of the Cafe had gathered at the

front of the building. Rick and Ly left by the side entrance.

A speeding car came to a halt while the two men exit the Cafe.

"Get in!" the female driver yelled when the second gunman came running around the side of the Cafe and opened fire.

"You are?" Rick asked getting into the front seat as Ly got in the back.

"No time for introductions now," said the driver looking at the rear-view mirror and see the gunner getting into a Range-Rover.

The chase began, the gunner while leaning out the window of the Range-Rover and fired at the speeding car carrying Rick and Ly.

"Let me off at the next corner!" Rick suggested. The driver made a left turn and slowed the car, Rick got out with the silencer attached to his gun, he waited.

As the Range-Rover made the turn, Rick fired two shots, the first hit the gunner, and he fell back into his seat, the second bullet hit the driver, the Ranger hit the edge of the sidewalk, then flipped over on its side.

Rick walked to the over-turned Range-Rover. And secure the kill with a bullet to the foreheads of the gunner and driver.

The car that picked up Rick and Ly Ling from the Cafe, reversed, and stopped beside the overturn Ranger.

"Shall we go?" the female driver asked.

"Yes, we should," replied Rick, getting into the front seat of the vehicle.

"Your friend Ly left this for you," said the driver handing Rick a piece of paper with the words "Be in touch" written on it along with a phone number.

"As to your earlier question, my name is Marie DeVos," said the woman driver.

"Thanks for turning up when you did," Rick Drago said appreciatively.

"I didn't just turn up; I've been following those two guys for a couple of days," Marie said.

"The Hijiri," Rick began to say.

Before he could finish the question, Marie showed him her credentials.

"The Hijiri arrived here today, the man traveling with him is of interests to many people and agencies."

"When and where the Hijiri will give his speech?" Rick asked.

"It's a spiritual gathering at King Baudouin Stadium, on Avenue de Marathon 135, the day after tomorrow. The stadium holds over 50,000 people and the tickets are sold out," Marie replied.

"Ling didn't say where he was going, did he?"

"No, he only left that piece of paper I gave to you," said Marie. "What do you think he'll do?"

"I think he'll kill Kim Ching if the opportunity arises," Rick said.

"Where are you staying?" Marie asked, somewhat prying.

"The NH Collection Brussels Grand Sablon," Rick Drago replied.

"I'll drop you off on my way to headquarters."

"Where can I rent a car?" Rick Drago queried.

"No need to do that, I'll take you where you want to go," Marie assured him.

"And what's that going to cost me?"

Marie smiled and said. "I'm sure you'll think of something."

"I'm already thinking about it," Rick informed her.

"You should get rested after your long flight and the activities of today," said Marie when she stopped in front of the hotel. "Give me your phone!"

Rick handed her the phone. "Call me after you've rested!" suggest Marie while she put her phone number into his phone.

"I'm in suite 410," said Rick getting out of the car and watched as Marie drove away.

In his suite. He took a shower, and before getting into bed, he checked the windows and the surroundings in the street below.

In the distance, a celebration was taking place with a beautiful display in the sky.

Rick then went to bed.

The telephone rang. He reached for it. The operator's voice was professionally brisk. "Good evening! A lady was on her way up to your suite."

Someone tapped on the door. Rick rose on his elbows, he slipped out of bed and put on the hotel bathrobe, then open the door to Marie DeVos, she hooded her eyes and pursed her lips into a smile.

Only then he realizes he didn't tie the waistband, and the front of the robe was open, revealing his manhood.

"There's a gathering of dignitaries who will be entertained this evening by the host of the spiritual event. I have two tickets for us to attend," Marie explained for being there at the moment.

Rick stepped to aside and allowed Marie to enter his suite.

He then disappeared into the bathroom; moments later, he returned fully dress.

"Shall we go?"

"Yes. Lets," Marie agreed. "When I first got here, I thought you would pay me before I did anything for you."

They both laughed as they left the suite.

"You will get pay," Rick Drago confirmed to her.

"I'm very much looking forward to my payday," she said.

Rick and Marie arrived at the function, and things were in full swing, a long buffet table, serving many patrons.

He prowled restlessly, integrating himself into the scene, getting a sense of it. As he always did when entering a place for the first time.

Rick sought the location of exits and stairways. If trouble broke, there wouldn't be time to search for a way out.

A waiter was carrying a tray with glasses of white and red wine; Marie took a glass of red.

"Any Whiskey?" Rick asked.

"At the bar, sir," replied the waiter.

The Hijiri wasn't hard to find, Rick saw the two large Japanese bodyguards standing at the side of a table, while the Hijiri chatted with a man wearing a red turban while a woman sat nearby.

Looking around, Rick didn't see Lucas Connors/Kim Ching.

"I don't see our man of interest," Marie continued. "Do you know the woman sitting with the Hijiri?"

"I think her name's Elizabeth Carson, an

interpreter for the Hijiri on this trip."

"In the far corner over your left shoulder, look and tell me, what do you see?"

Rick took a couple of steps forward, turned to face Marie, and sees none other than Ly Ling in a bearded disguise sipping a glass of wine. "Should we say hello?"

"No, I'm sure he saw us when we arrived."

"We should get a table!" suggested Marie.

"Agreed."

Marie and Rick found a vacant table near the entrance and sat down.

"Let's get something to eat from the buffet table!" Marie suggested.

After standing in line for what seemed like an eternity, they reached the buffet table and took a plate of food.

Rick choose the grilled salmon with fresh vegetables while Marie choose a mixed cold plate comprise ham, cheese, and raw vegetables, then returned to their table and sat down.

Leaving Marie sitting at the table. He got up and surveyed the mingling patrons of the Middle East, Western, Asian, and Arabic spiritual seekers.

They are representatives of Governments, dealers, traders; It's a strange gathering of people from the four corners of the globe.

Arabic men dressed with the latest style suits

from the west, their heads with the usual head-wear. At this gathering, few women are in attendance. Another extensive scan of the room turned up no sign of Kim Ching/Lucas Connors. he returned to the table, sat down with Marie, and finish eating his meal.

"It doesn't look like Kim Ching will attend this event," Rick observed. "Some guests are leaving."

"According to the invitation, the event is only for four hours, finishing at eleven pm."

He looked at his watch.

"The time is now ten-fifteen."

A waiter approached the table and handed a note to Rick. On the piece of paper was written. "Will be in touch! He's not here."

Rick and Marie looked to where they had seen Ly standing, and he was nowhere in sight.

"We should leave!" Rick suggested.

"It's still early, and you're all rested. What would you like to do?"

"This is my first visit to Brussels; I would like to see what the nightlife has to offer."

"Do you gamble?"

"I play poker, Texas hold'em."

"Then, we go to the Virage Casino!"

After a couple of hours, Marie and Rick left the Casino after cashing in their winning. He did well at the poker table with winning over a thousand American dollars, and Marie pocketed a few hundred Euro notes from the slot machines.

"Would you like to come up for a nightcap?" he asked when Marie stopped the car in front of the hotel.

"If you need me to keep driving you around for the time, you'll be visiting here; I have to collect the first payment tonight."

Marie parked the car, and they entered the lobby of the hotel. At the front desk, there's a message for Rick from Michael Strong in London.

Drago took the envelope with the message to his suite and read it aloud. "Lo Don Chung, head of C.M.L.F, arrived in Haiti yesterday at three o'clock in the evening local time.

Diana Mercer is on a flight from Toronto to Trinidad & Tobago.

From the port of Hamilton, Ontario, a cargo ship carrying a unique article is due to arrive in Port Au Prince, Haiti.

The Manifest says the container will deliver to L.D.C. International Industries."

Marie listens while he read the message from Michael, then went into the bathroom, returning moments later wearing the hotel bathrobe that Drago was wearing when she came to pick him up earlier. Drago burned the paper after reading the message.

"Who's Michael?" Marie questioned Rick.

"He's ex-MI6. Unofficially still works for them and us."

"And Diana! Who is she? And what does she has to do with the prototype?"

"I believe she's down there representing her step-father's interest in the delivery of that half of the prototype."

"Is she the person who shipped it?"

"Not sure, she could be there in Trinidad to collect money owed to her dead step-father David Mercier."

Drago got up from the chair and undressed, heading for the bathroom.

Marie stood in his way with the front of the robe open, giving a glimpse of her two lovely breasts and a flat stomach.

She stood like that, letting Rick's eyes sucked in the perfection of her body. Marie then breathed, her nipples rubbed against the robe and hardened, warmly inviting to be caressed.

He took her in his arms, kissed her breast moving his lips up along her neck, they lips meet, and he felt the heat of Marie. Her hand searched and found his manhood.

Marie arched her shoulders and let the robe fall to the rug. She then jumps and wrapped her legs around his waist as he put his arms around her and stumble onto the bed.

Both of them had a fulfilling night of lovemaking. They took an early morning swim in the hotel pool before having a breakfast of eggs and fruits. Later, at the breakfast table, a flight itinerary was delivered to Rick by courier.

"What time is your flight?"

"A private Jet this evening at seventeen hundred."

"Okay, I know the airstrip," said Marie, with a big smile on her face. "You have time to give me my final payment for services rendered," she teased.

"How much cash do I owe you? And what makes you say the final payment? I could return," he informed her.

"You don't owe me any cash, silly. And are you planning on coming back here to visit me?"

"No promises, I'll stay in touch."

"You say that to all the girls you meet in the countries you've visited?"

"No. I don't."

"I'm flattered that you think of me that way," Marie said smiling.

After breakfast. Marie went to her office. Two hours later, she returned and stayed with Rick. She took him on a sight-seeing tour of Belgium.

Then later, she took Rick to the private airstrip and watched while he got on board the plane.

She waited until the plane took off before getting back into her car and drove away.

Rick took the opportunity of the flight to catch up on a little shut-eye.

Upon arriving in Haiti. Waiting for him at the airstrip was Jane Blackwell.

"How was your flight?" Jane asked.

"Long. what's the latest on the ship?"

"The ship arrived this morning, and we had it delayed on entering the port; it's at anchor outside of the harbor."

"Good. Can the container with the article be easily identified?"

"Yes, it has a fragile yellow sticker on it. The General man in customs and excise working out of Hamilton, Ontario placed the marker there."

"Can you drive by the harbor? I'll like to have a look at where the ship's anchored."

"What are you thinking?" Jane questioned.

"After I look at the ship, I'll let you know."

In Trinidad, Diana checked into the Hilton hotel for her stay on the Island.

After looking at where the ship was. Rick decided.

"Can you get me a rubber dingy with a small outboard motor?"

"Of course," Jane replied. "What time do you

need it?"

"I need it for tonight. And you have to accompany me."

"What about the promise you made to me on your last visit?"

"I don't remember making a promise to you."

"You don't remember kissing me either?"

"How could I forget those sensuous lips of yours?"

"You have a suite at the same hotel you stayed on your last visit," Jane said. "I'll take you there and check with you later."

"Okay."

From his hotel suite. He put a call through to the General.

They diverted the phone call to Sam Harris.

"Hey, Rick. How's the weather in Haiti?" Sam asked when he answered the phone.

"Hot. what can you tell me about the container?"

"The container was at the bow of the ship, second from the port side and third from the top with a sticker you will recognize. There's a car in the container and under the back seat of that car you'll find the item," Sam explained.

"Give my regards to the General!" Rick said, then hung up the phone before getting a reply from Sam.

Rick then called Dan McCall, the acting head

of the AWB division, and brought him up to date on the missing piece of the prototype.

"Your orders are to destroy the item quick and safe!" Dan stated.

"I will board the ship tonight and retrieve the item."

"The General is here in New York undergoing tests on his liver."

"I wish him good health," Rick said before turning off the phone.

At eleven that night. Rick, in the company of Jane, headed for the area where he had entered the water. It was about half a mile from the anchored ship.

Slowly he reached the ship and tied the rubber dingy to the anchor chain.

The time is eleven forty-five, that's the time watches change, when the midnight shift replaces the eight to twelve watch, a perfect time for him to go onboard the vessel.

The handing over of paperwork, giving information on tank soundings, and other things happening during the night shift.

Rick used the chain and climbed aboard the ship. He has no problem finding the container and going inside.

Rick carried the replica of the prototype which the General had sent to him on the first trip he made to Bermuda and Haiti.

Chapter Ten

He removed the object from under the back seat of the vehicle, taking the replica from the watertight bag he carried on his back, and placed it under the seat, a few minutes later he was back in the rubber dingy with the real prototype.

He untied the dingy and paddle away from the ship, then started the motor and headed a considerable distance from the shoreline and stop.

Rick took the tube of metal-eating paste from a pocket on his wet-suit and squeezed the contents onto the prototype and watched while it liquified. Then he let the metal and the sack slip away in the sea.

Moments later, he returned to the pickup point where Jane was waiting for him.

"How did it go?" Jane asked while Rick deflated the rubber dingy.

"I had no problem, the hunk of metal that was once a dangerous item was at the bottom of the sea."

"Great," said Jane, giving Rick a hand in storing the dingy in the trunk of her car.

The next morning, they give the ship in port the all-clear to depart, allowing the anchored vessel to enter and discharged its cargo.

One particular thing interested Drago and Jane, and she has selected a team to follow the container to its final destination, where Drago was hoping to put an end to this threat from Lo Don Chung and the C.M.L.F group of Fanatics.

Back in his suite at the hotel, he checked the messages from Dan and then Michael.

He had left the phone behind when he visited the ship. Rick checked the message from Dan. It was a video from Brussels showing the bodies of three men found in the penthouse suite of a hotel.

The body identified as Kim Ching tortured. The thumb and fourth finger removed from both of his hands. Stabbed wounds in both of his knees and a tiny hole in the center of his heart. "Look at this," Rick said.

Jane sat beside Rick she watched the footage and read the description displayed on the phone.

"You think Ly Wing did that to Kim Ching?"

"Ly had to restore his family name," said Drago. "He's sending a message to let others know that his family was not to be touched."

Rick Drago then read the message from Michael.

"Leaving for Barbados on the 13th of July will stay there until the end of the crop over festival with my friend LH."

Dan McCall was now in charge of the A.W.B section within the service; he's the only one that Rick Drago will informed about his actions.

Drago calls Dan and brings him up to date with the progress on the prototype.

"Joanne left for Barbados yesterday, a friend invited her to the festival there," said Dan.

"I will go to Barbados when this is over, Michael is also going to the festival there, and I promised to join him."

"Michael?" Dan quizzed.

"Yes. Our man in London."

"Okay," said Dan McCall.

"Michael and his buddy, the race car driver, will attend, and he asked me to join them."

"Then, you see Joanne on the Island."

"Maybe, I'll keep in touch."

Both men hung up their phones. Jane stayed with Drago in his suite until the next morning, after breakfast she called a member of her team at the port and found out that the ship had entered and began to discharge the cargo."

In Barbados, Chuck picked up Joanne at the Sir Grantley Adams International Airport and took her to the Beach hotel where he had made a reservation for her to stay during her visit to the Island.

Chuck planned his two week's vacation from his job to fit-in with Joanne's visit to the Island,

and the Crop-Over festivities.

Now, while Chuck and Joanne ride in the elevator with the bell-boy, she lay her head on Chuck's chest as he puts his arms around Joanne and squeezed her.

Chuck tip the bell-boy after he opens the door and put the luggage in the suite, Joanne took the sandals off her feet and began undressing as Chuck remove his shirt.

Joanne turned, got on her knees and removed the belt from his pants. The long-awaited love session between Joanne and Chuck lasts well into the night, after which both of them fell asleep, waking up hungry they ordered a cold plate and salad from room service.

"I now know why so many women come to these Islands," Joanne said.

"Does that mean you'll be coming back?" Chuck queried.

"Every chance I get, I'll be here," said Joanne."

"Good," Chuck said. "Do you want to go out?"

"No, let's stay in tonight, we have plenty of time to go out."

A smiling Joanne sits on the lap of Chuck and kisses him, then whisper in his ear. "You're an animal in bed."

He smiled and kissed her tenderly on her lips. "You are so beautiful. I wanted to make love to you all night."

"You have three weeks to do that."

"I will need lots of energy."

They laughed and hugged each other.

It's five in the evening, George notified Jane that they have loaded the container on a truck and were heading for the receiver's address.

"Let's go!" Jane commanded.

"Is he there?"

"No, he's not. The container were on a truck and leaving the port."

"The L.D.C International Industries, was it accessible from the beach?" Drago queried.

"No, why do you ask?"

"Want to be sure all exits were covered, and I don't want Lo Don Chung getting away."

"we will block all exits," Jane assured Drago there's nothing for him to worry.

"How about the security at the building?"

"One-armed guard was at the gate, not sure how many are inside."

"How many agents you have on this operation?" Rick Drago asked.

"A team of six, after the truck left the port, we intercept and remove the driver, an agent was now driving the vehicle."

"Lo Don Chung was to be stopped at all costs, dead or alive."

Entering through the gate of L.D.C International Industries, the team took out the guard.

Rick, Jane, and George approach from the back, the agents made sure they blocked all exits from the building.

The early evening was hot, breathlessly humid, no longer sunny. Big dark clouds filled the sky where the sun once was only a few minutes ago. It would rain, like most of the tropical Islands, rain for a few minutes then stops.

George lead the way up the back stairs heading for the office with Jane and Rick following. Suddenly, gunfire erupted below, then an explosion.

George opened the door of the office, a hail of bullets greeted him, the big man rolled firing while he did, one gunman drops to one knee when Jane fired off Six rounds finding their mark bringing the other gunman down.

Rick glimpsed Lo Don Chung going out the door and fired a few rounds in a cross pattern, hoping to stop him from getting away.

The warehouse is on fire from the explosion that happened earlier, while Drago found a trail of blood leading away from the office. He knew the blood was from Lo Don Chung.

Drago, moving quickly, caught sight of the Japanese holding his left side with an attaché case under his right arm.

"End of the road Chung, stop!" commanded Rick.

"Mr. Rick , my worthy adversary, is it you?" queried Chung without turning around.

"On your knees!"

Lo Don Chung refused the command of Drago; Instead, he turned around in a swift motion.

The marksmanship of Rick came into play when he fired. The bullet found its mark in the center of Chung's forehead. He was dead before his body hit the floor.

Jane and George joined Rick.

Jane then took the case from the dead man's hand.

"How bad is it?" he asked George, seeing the bloodstain on his shoulder.

"I took one above the vest, it's only a flesh wound," replied George.

"He'll live."

In the distance, the sound of firetrucks approaching the burning building.

"I have to get out of here."

"George will drive you to your hotel, I have to stay and explain to the local authorities what happened here," Jane informed him.

"Okay, I have to take the case," Rick suggested.

Jane handed the attaché case to Rick. "I'll

come by later and pick it up."

Rick knew Jane was only letting him know that she'll come and see him later.

In his suite, Rick called the Embassy and schedule a picked up time in fifteen minutes.

"Under no circumstances should the driver get out of the car and enter the hotel, the driver should wait to be contacted by me," Rick said to the intelligence officer he spoke too.

Rick took a chair and jammed it against the book, then placed the case behind the mini-bar at the back of the small fridge before going into the shower.

Thirty minutes later, Rick was at the Embassy with the attaché case having it examined before opening it. He took this precaution, not knowing if the case has a booby trap for safety from unauthorized tampering.

Inside the case, the names of prominent people in offices around the globe.

Diana is not among them. David Mercier's name is there next to a payment made for four hundred thousand American dollars, dated the day before he was the victim of a hit-and-run accident.

Rick called Dan McCall and informed him of the situation in Haiti.

"Operation ISLE, went into effect last night, waiting on the information you recover from Lo

Don Chung to wrap it up," said Dan.

"Everything's on its way to you through the usual channels," Rick continued. "I'm on my way to Barbados in a day or two."

"Diana was staying at the Beach hotel or something like that," said Dan. "Do you want her contact number?"

"No, I'll find her."

In Barbados, Michael Strong and his good friend, Lewis, arrived by private jet from London, England. After clearing customs and immigration boarded the limousine and headed for the Villa at The Royal Westmoreland.

Michael calls Rick Drago.

"Hi Michael," said Rick, answering the phone.

"I'm in Barbados."

"Where are you staying?"

"That's why I'm calling, no need for you to book hotel reservations, there's a room here at the villa for you."

"I haven't booked at any hotel yet, and I wasn't sure of my arrival time on the Island."

"The villa has five rooms, three of them are still empty."

"I have to book a flight, will let you know the time of arrival."

"Okay. I understand Diana's here on the

Island."

"Yes, she is there. I'm not sure where she's staying."

"See you soon."

Arriving at Sir Grantley Adams airport in Barbados, Rick presented his credentials and bypass immigration and customs.

Michael Strong meets him and takes him to the villa at The Royal Westmoreland.

A small gathering of Lewis' friends were at the villa having a few drinks and laughs.

Settling in the room made available for him, Rick called his friend Inspector Brown.

"Didn't know you were coming to the Island," Brown said.

"My friend Michael from London was here for the crop over festival and ask if I would join him."

"Where are you staying?"

"We are at The Royal Westmoreland."

"In the upper-class neighborhood."

"How long will you be staying?"

"Until the end of the festival."

"Joanne is here, and she's staying at The Beach Hotel."

"How's the Chief of police and his wife?"

"The old man is still going strong. Why don't you call him? He'd love to hear from you."

"I'll do that," Rick replied.

"I hear music in the background."

"Yes, some friends of Lewis are here to welcome him back to the Island."

"We should get together for a night on the town before you leave!"

"Cool. Whenever you're free."

"Okay, I'll stay in touch," Brown said, and the receiver went dead.

Rick then took a shower and joined the other guest. Six young ladies and two men, along with Lewis and Michael, with Rick making six to five.

"About time," said Michael when Rick entered the room. "The ladies are eager to meet you."

Michael did the introduction between Rick and Lewis, then to the ladies who had gathered around them.

The social gathering lasted late into the night. Rick retired to his room in the company of Kayla, a young, long-legged black British model with a chiseled ass, a pair of beautiful breasts, held in place with a halter top.

Kayla was magnificent. She removed the fastener holding the one shoulder strap that held her dress in place and let it fall at her feet. The splendor of her curve body dazzled Drago.

Rick embraced her, she made an armful. The aroma of her naked was like nothing he'd ever experience.

He found the catch to her halter, after a

moment or two, it came undone and her breast tumble free, her nipple was inviting, and he nibbled on them.

Moaning, Kayla played with his head, neck, and felt the muscles in his massive arms and shoulders.

She moved away from Rick while he took off his clothes, Kayla then lay her naked body on the bed, legs slightly open. She looked at his aroused body, standing at the edge of the bed.

Kayla smiled at him and whispered." Take me!"

He went between her parted legs, and it left him breathless, the firmness of her sleek body.

They had a beautiful session of sexual activity lasted into the early morning hours of the next day.

Rick and Kayla became inseparable in the days that followed. The only time Rick saw Joanne is at Inspector Brown's dinner party.

Joanne attended the party alone. She reached the home of Brown before Drago and showed disappointment when he walked in with Kayla holding his hand.

"How are you, Rick?" Joanne sheepishly asked.

"I'm good," replied Rick. "This is Kayla Grandison."

The two women shook hands and exchanged pleasantries then Joanne gave Kayla the look of envy.

Rick Drago notices the uneasiness of Joanne.

"How's Chuck?" Rick asked, trying to break tension between the two women. .

"He's Okay."

"This is my friend Michael from London and his buddy Lewis also from London and their dates," Rick informed moving on to greet Inspector Brown who is standing with the Chief of police and their wives.

The Islands elite law enforcement, judges, lawyers, and police officers attended the dinner party.

A few days later, Rick called Dan and received the news about the death of General Applewaite.

"When did this happen?" asked Drago.

"A few days ago," said Dan. "Have you seen Diana?"

"Yes, I saw her at Inspector Brown dinner party."

"When are you leaving the Island?"

"I'm here for another seven days."

"I'll like you to stop over in Canada and attend the General funeral!"

"I thought he would be buried in the states?"

"No, I understand he wished to be laid to rest in Canada."

"Okay."

"I know you enjoy working out in the field, someone has to take over the general duties, and I think you and Joanne could do that until a replacement found."

"From what you're saying, I gather he had no deputy or assistant to succeed him."

"That's correct," Dan said.

"What about Sam Harris?" Rick asked.

"He has no background in intelligence work. I believe the General would send Sam here to do his training. I came across a file with a recommendation for Sam Harris."

"What about Diana Mercer? She worked closely with the General, and we found she did nothing wrong," Rick continued. "She's also here on the Island for the festivities."

"Did you talked with her there on the Island?"

"No, I didn't, Michael had a chat with her at a function he attended with his friend Lewis."

"Ly Ling tried to get in touch with you, and when he didn't reach you, he called the General private number, they transferred the call to me as per the General instruction."

"Okay, the phone Ly had was no longer active, and the contact number I had to reach him was on that phone. Did he say where I can reach him?"

"No. I have the number of the phone Ly Ling used to make the call."

"Maybe he'll attend the General funeral to pay his respect," Rick said.

"I'll give you the number, you can call him if you wish," Dan said.

Rick passed on the news of the General death to Michael Strong, a few days later Rick and Michael are on a flight from Barbados to Canada.

Joanne and Diana arrived in Canada a day later in time to attend the Generals funeral service.

The intelligence community was respectfully represented.

Ly Ling made the trip to Toronto paying his respect to the General, he checked into a hotel close to the Pearson International Airport.

"Mr. Rick, how good it is to see you," said Ly Ling, as he approaches Drago standing on the steps of the chapel with Michael.

"The feeling is mutual," Rick replied.

"Hello, Michael," said Ly. " I hope Mr. Rick has explained the reason for my action against you back in London."

Michael turned and walked into the chapel without replying to the Ly Ling query.

"I suspect from his reaction; you said nothing to him."

"There's nothing to say."

"Should I be caution in his presence?"

"You can have a talk with him and explain why you did it!"

A black Escalade with tinted windows stopped in front of the chapel. No one got out. Then two security guards approached the vehicle, one at the front, the other from the back.

From the steps, Rick and Ling watch as the Escalade slowly drove away.

"Friends of yours?" Rick asked, making a mental note of the license plates.

"I came alone, no friends or family," replied Ling.

The two men then entered the chapel and stayed at the back as the service began.

After the service, he asked Sam Harris to run a check on the license plate he took on the Escalade.

The results came back when they were at the gravesite. The vehicle is register to Riku Amano.

He's the nephew of the Japanese consulate-general in Toronto.

Rick shared the information with Ly Ling.

The same vehicle is at the cemetery where the body of the General is laid to rest.

Paul and Bob, the bodyguards of the late General, advanced towards the vehicle. When they got close, the Escalade drove away.

The next morning, Rick accompanied Michael

to the airport for his flight back to London. The two agents shook hands and said their goodbyes.

Rick then went to Scarborough and entered the T.A Canadian Telecommunication building and for the first time, visited the office of General Tom Applewaite, which was located on the fifth floor and takes up the entire area.

Sam then gave Rick and Joanne the tour of the firm.

At the south end of the floor, there's a short flight of stairs that leads to another section with two doors.

Another floor built inside the fifth floor, not noticeable from the outside. Joanne stopped and looked at the structure.

"In case you're wondering. That's the General and his private secretary offices," Sam continued. "Come on! Let's meet her."

Entering the office, the secretary got up from behind her desk.

"Gina, this is Rick Drago and Joanne McCall, they will give us a hand until the replacement for the General comes," said Sam Harris.

Handshakes and greeting from everyone. Gina is a tall, buxom redhead, standing over five feet wearing a pair of glasses on the bridge of her nose.

She sat back down behind her desk and gave Joanne the once over. Sam then took them to the

General's office, where the two bodyguards, Paul and Bob, are sitting at a desk.

The two big men got up and greeted Rick with a handshake.

"Boys. This is Joanne McCall. Joanne, meet Paul and Bob." Sam introduced the bodyguards.

He then continued to bring Rick and Joanne up to date with the surroundings.

It's entirely bulletproof and has an express lift that goes directly to the basement, capable of carrying six people.

"When was the last time Paul and Bob had time off?"

"I can't remember."

"This is a perfect time to give them a vacation."

"Great idea."

"Your first official duty, Joanne," Rick implied.

Chapter Eleven

Later that day, orders came in for Sam Harris to report to Camp Peary, better known as "The Farm" the following day to begin his training.

A few days later, a distress signal from Bermuda. The office was under attack by armed people in the early morning hours, after it was over five people was wounded, they have reported no deaths.

Computers and other sensitive information was missing and believed to be in the hands of the attackers.

Rick Drago was once again back in Bermuda,

and Maggie was at the airport to greet him.

"I knew you'd come," said Maggie, reaching up and kissing Drago on his cheek.

"I miss you too," Drago replied.

"Where is your luggage?"

"I didn't have time to pack anything; I hurried here."

"You care, don't you?"

"How did they penetrate your top-level security?"

"Someone tried to hack us the day before the attack; We block whoever it was, now this happened."

"It's a good thing that you didn't attend the Generals funeral. It was smart of you to let your dad represent the family at the ceremony."

"I had nothing to do with it; my dad insisted I stay here and let him make the trip to Canada hoping to see some old friends while he's there."

"How many were they?"

"We were blind about 30 seconds, no power until the emergency unit in the basement kicked in, with the help of CCTV, we counted five people entered."

"Did you see any of their faces?"

"Yes, we have two of them. Both are Japanese, Koki Amano, and Yuto Akagi."

Rick watched while Maggie display the two images on the large monitor. He then gave

Maggie his cell phone with Ly Ling's contact number.

"Dial this number and put it on speakerphone!" Drago exclaimed.

"Hello, Ling here, who's calling?"

"Rick here."

"Ah, Rick, I was about to call for an update on those people at the cemetery."

"What can you tell me about Koki Amano and Yuto Akagi?"

"A moment, Mr. Rick," Ly Ling said.

"Who's Ling?" Maggie asked.

"He's the head of Japan fraud squad, he and I first meet in London in a peculiar situation."

"Koki Amano is the oldest brother of Riku Amano and Yuto Akagi was close friends from school days, they are members of an elite task force here in Japan," Ling said. "Why do you ask?"

"I asked because they broke into our office in Bermuda and took something belonging to the Agency."

"Hold on, let me do a little checking!"

Maggie punched in the two names through Pearson International airport and waited. Results came back; the two men had boarded a flight for Hong Kong that very day.

"Get me on the next flight to Hong Kong!" Drago exclaimed.

Maggie gave the order to one of her assistants.

"The two of them are on leave from their duties and won't be back until the following week," said Ling.

"They are on a flight from Canada to Hong Kong, and it departed here this morning."

"Anything I can do to help?"

"I'm on my way to Hong Kong, send any information you gather to this office until I arrive!"

"I will meet you on arrival," Ly Ling said.

The connection went dead when both men hang up.

"Can he be trusted?" Maggie asked.

"Yes."

"I'll prepare a diplomatic paper for you to take," Maggie said. "You can use the same room as the last time."

Rick didn't object. Diplomatic status comes in handy at certain times when you are traveling. He went up the stairs and entered the room.

Everything in the room was the way he left it. He smiled to himself, remembering the last time he was there.

A knock on his room door. Wearing only a shirt not buttoned, exposing his chest and an underwear. "Come in!" Rick said expecting it to be Maggie, but it was her secretary with the flight information.

The stunning brunette stared in awe, with her mouth open at Rick's muscular body.

"Here is your itinerary for the flight to Hong Kong," she said, handing the paper with shaky hands to him, and her eyes fixed on his waist as if wishing for the boxer briefs to fall to his feet.

Their hands touch when he took the paper from her, and she backed away from him.

"Why are you shaking? Don't be afraid!"

"I'm not afraid."

"Then, why?" Rick didn't finish what he was about to say before the woman went out and close the door.

Rick tossed the itinerary on the bed and notice a tiny slip of paper with something written on it, Drago read the note.

"Here is my number, please call me anytime! Annabelle."

Drago then entered the number on his cell phone and flushed the paper down the toilet.

After taking a shower, Drago called Dan and bring him up to date on what had happened at the office.

"When are you leaving for Hong Kong?"

"In the morning," Drago replied.

"Our man in Hong Kong will pick you up at the airport."

"Ly Ling offered to pick me up, and I accepted. He promises to keep tabs on two of the people responsible for breaking into the office."

Yuto Akagi walked up the three flights of stairs and enter room C-22. He wasn't sure if he and his friend Koki was followed from the airport.

Instead of going home, Yuto stayed at a hotel for a couple of days. He dropped the flight bag on the floor and checked the entire room, and then he stretched out on the bed.

It was a long flight from Bermuda, and the days before heading back to Hong Kong, he didn't get much sleep.

Lying in the bed on his back, he thought about the mistake they made at the office in Bermuda, not thinking about the emergency power source coming on so quickly and making them leave before the task was complete.

Yuto woke up from the noise coming from outside. Looking at the watch still on his hand, he realized he had slept for three hours.

The sound he heard came from a truck backfire on the street outside his room window.

Ly Ling meet Rick at the airport, then they headed to the hotel where Yuto's staying. From the diplomatic pouch, Rick retrieves his gun and harness.

At the front desk, Ly Ling shows his

credentials to the clerk and asks for the room number of Yuto Akagi.

"He's in room C-22," replied the clerk.

"Passkey!" command Ling.

Rick and Ling took the lift to the third floor. Don't disturb sign was hanging on the door of C-22.

Ly Ling softly knocks on the door, hearing no answer he opened the door, they entered.

The room was searched, pillowcases, sheets ripped apart, contents of a bag are on the carpet.

Rick and Ly drew their weapons and moved through the room. A large brass chandelier and fan in the ceiling, two tiny empty whiskey bottles from the minibar on a table with the small lamp lit, and the drawers left open.

They looked at each other and nodded in the bathroom's direction. Yuto's body was in the bathtub.

A professional had tortured Yuto Akagi before being shot at close range, a single bullet wound in the center of his forehead.

Rick looked around the room, nothing. He searches under the bathroom sink and under the light shades.

He then stood in the bathroom with a disgusting and disappointing look on his face.

Like the person or persons before him, Rick found nothing on the body of Agaki or in the room.

"Whatever they took from the office in Bermuda seems of importance to someone," Ly Ling stated.

"Yes, what about his traveling partner?" Rick asked.

"I know where to find him; I have to get the forensic team here. You should take my car and go to your hotel and wait for me!"

Rick checked into the hotel and made a call to the Embassy. Rick text Ly Ling and gave him the number of the suite since he had checked in using an alias. He then rented a Range Rover to be dropped off at the hotel.

It was just after eight and the sun changed its color to a bright red, Ly Ling got out of an unmarked police car and entered the hotel lobby where Rick had checked into earlier.

Darkness is now in the skies, the few clouds are now tinted red by the setting sun as Ly Ling, and Rick left the hotel suite.

"I don't want you to get into trouble with your superiors, I have a rental, and will follow you. When we get there, leave," said Drago.

Ly Ling and Rick parked the vehicles one block over from the place they're going.

Arriving at the address, Ling insisted on staying, and they walked to the house. The structure is a two-story building that looks more like a prison than a house.

"This place was a safe house," Ling explained.

"It doesn't look that safe to me," he replied. "I don't think you should be here."

Rick picked the old lock and entered. The place dimly lit with one lamp on the desk, a laptop with a display on the screen.

A lit cigarette with other butts, and ashes are in an ashtray.

Rick heard the water in the bathroom running; he removes the UBS stick from the laptop, punched in a code, and hits the delete button destroying the hard-drive and all its contents.

Moving to the bathroom, Rick wrapped the shower curtain around the man's head, applying a vise-like drip until the body went limp.

Rick then sat the man down in a chair. He secures the man's left foot to the left leg of the chair and the right foot to the right with duct tape.

The two hands secured at the back of the chair with nylon tie-wraps. While Rick waited for the man to open his eyes, he searched the other rooms.

In the basement, Rick found a room with telecommunication equipment; he destroyed it before he left the premises, not wanting to attract attention until he's finished with the man strap in the chair.

Two slaps to the face given by Rick, one left the other right. The man slowly opens his eyes. He'd regain consciousness.

"Welcome back," Rick continued. " I hope you understand and speak English.

"Yes, I speak English. Who are you, and what do you want?"

"Who I am is not important," he said.

"American? What are you doing here?"

"I'll ask. You provide the answers truthfully!"

"Depends."

"Who gave you the order to break into the office in Bermuda?" asked Drago. "And before you say that you don't know what I'm talking about, we have your picture."

"My picture?"

"Yes, your picture and your friend Yuto Akagi, and that you're still alive could only mean that he didn't give you up after being tortured by someone before being shot to death."

"Killed? Yuto is dead?" asked Koki Amano.

"Yes, they found him at the hotel where he was staying and tortured him."

"I don't know who gave the order."

"I have no time for this, I'm asking you nicely. You should cooperate with me because Yuto didn't give you up; that's not to say the next person on the list won't."

"I truly don't know."

Rick knocked the chair over on its back, he took the ice bucket, filled it with water, and place a towel over Koki's face and poured the water on his face.

Koki didn't give Rick any information about who had hired him and his friend Yuto, supplying them with return tickets to Bermuda.

After the water tortured didn't prove productive, Rick then shot Koki in the temple, set the building ablaze, and left.

He went to the Embassy and scrambled a call to AWB headquarters.

"Nothing from this end about who gave the order to break into the office in Bermuda," said Drago to Dan when he answered the phone.

"Nothing?" Dan asked.

"Both dead-ends," replied Rick.

"When are you going back to Canada?"

"Not sure, did Joanne get anything new from Maggie in Bermuda?"

"No. I asked Maggie about her employees, and she assured me they all can be trusted, even the replacements that worked there over the summer holidays were young recruits from the farm."

"There's a leak someplace," Rick assumed.

"Did you receive any help from Ling?"

"He provided the addresses of the two dead ends," Rick replied.

"Okay."

Rick hung up the phone and was about to leave when a tall, distinguished man in a dark pinstripe suit walked into the room.

It had to be the deputy chief of mission, Angel Cross, with an outstretched hand.

"Glad you're still here," said Cross when he shook Rick's hand. "I'm Angel Cross, deputy chief.

"I know who you are," Rick Drago said, letting Cross know that he's well informed about him.

Rick Drago doesn't care too much for politicians, while most of them are full of hot air with no substance to anything they say.

Angel Cross, followed by a stubby Japanese man dressed in a grey suit and smoking a Kiseru-pipe, enters the room.

"This is Arata Furuta, he's from the Ministry of Defense, and would like our help," Cross explained.

"Our help?" Rick asked with a puzzled look on his face.

"Shall we go to my office!" suggests Cross leading the way from the communication room.

The three men entered Cross's office and sat down.

"It seems that two members of Mr. Furuta elite

team has gone missing, and he would like our help in locating them," Angel Cross said.

"What do you mean gone missing? And why come here for information?" Rick asked.

"We share intel. Him and me," said Cross. "And knowing you just arrived from the west, I thought you might have heard something."

Rick studied Cross and Futura and wondered what type of intel they share.

At that moment, Rick cell phone ring.

"I have to take this," said Rick when leaving the office.

"Yuto and Koki came back a couple of days ago, and no one has seen them since that time," said Furuta.

"Why do you think our man Rick may help you?"

"He arrived the day after; he could have followed them here."

"Officially. He's here on a special assignment. Hush-hush," Cross said.

"Two of my most trusted men haven't been heard from in a long time, it's not like them not to check-in with their superiors," Futura said to Cross.

"When are you coming back?" Joanne asked.

"Not sure. Is everything okay?" Rick asked with a concern tone.

"Everything's good."

"And the job?"

"Things are running smoothly," Joanne assured him.

"Great. I know you'll do a great job. I'll let you know when I'm on my way back."

Drago hanged up the phone after talking with Joanne and immediately called Michael Strong in London.

Hi, Michael," Rick said when Michael answered the phone.

"Hi Mate, how's the Asian weather? And the women?"

"The weather has been good, the women? Haven't got around to them yet," Rick said. "I need you to run a check on a couple of guys for me."

"No problem."

"Angel Cross and Arata Futura. When can you get back to me with the information?"

"I'm on it, mate."

Rick walked back into the office, Cross and Futura seemed to have a disagreeable discussion and stopped at the sight of him.

"Sorry for the interruption," Rick said.

"No need for that, I know operatives in the field are always on the go," said Cross.

"You get out in the field, much?" Rick raised a brow.

At that moment, Futura cell phone buzz. After

answering the call, he said to Cross.

"I'm needed at the office."

"Okay," Angel Cross replied.

The two men walked out of Cross's office, leaving Rick alone.

Reading the text, Michael sent him on his phone. It stated that Angel Cross and Arata Futura attended the same university in the USA and remained friends after graduating.

Cross returned to his office while Rick was leaving. "How much longer will you be staying?" Cross asked.

"I'm waiting for headquarters."

"How is the boss?" asked Cross, trying to make small talk with Rick, who wasn't about to become friendly with him. Knowing that someday he may have him in his sights at the end of his gun if he had anything to do with the Bermuda affair.

Maggie was someone Rick was very fond of, and anyone responsible for frightening or harming people he cares about. He delivers a message clear and understandable to back off.

"As far as I know, all is good."

Rick Drago entered the hallway and walked away. He heard the loud noise when Cross slam the door shut behind him.

Arriving at the office of the Ministry of Defense, Major General Ki Harada, the leader of his elite team, a tall skinny man met Futura.

"I just returned from the morgue," said the Major.

"What were you doing there?" Futura asked.

"We received information about two bodies with no identity papers and we investigated," the Major replied.

"And?" Futura asked.

"I identified one was Yuto Akagi, someone who knew what they were doing tortured him, a professional, perhaps," said the Major. "According to the examiner, it happened over sixty hours ago."

"What about the other?" asked Futura. "Koki Amano, what about him?"

"The body of the other person was so severely burned; we identify him through his dental records."

"Is it Koki?" Futura asked.

"Yes, it is Koki Amano," replied the Major, with sadness in his voice.

"Do you have any idea who did this to our men?" Futura asked.

"A foreigner, perhaps, American?"

"You're not thinking about the latest diplomat to arrive."

"And why not? He's not a pencil pusher, is he?"

"You should look elsewhere!"

"Why? You don't believe it was him?" queried the Major.

"It couldn't be him."

"And why not?" the Major questioned.

"Because Major, sixty hours ago, he was not here."

"Two of my best men, dead. And I do not understand what they were doing in the Caribbean?" the Major said.

"I'm hoping you'll explain that to me."

"The talk was, Koki and Yuto left to visit Koki's brother in the Caribbean. I knew it couldn't be true because his brother was in Canada."

"What are you going to do about the death of your men?"

"I've already begun looking for answers."

"Good. I'll see what I can find out through diplomatic channels," said Futura, shaking the Major hands. "Keep me up to date with your progress."

Rick Drago got into his rental Range Rover and drove away from the Embassy. Moments later, he spotted the vehicle tailing him.

Drago made a call to Ly Ling.

"Did you send a team to follow me?"

"No. I know better than to send any of my men to lose their lives foolishly," Ling replied.

"I picked up a tail when I left the Embassy."

"Where are you now?" Ly Ling asked.

"On Chrome Street four blocks west of the Embassy."

"I Will be there in a few minutes, stay on your present path!" Ly Ling said.

Minutes later, the high beam flash from Ling's car caught Drago's eye, and he flashes back. Rick turns off the street and watches as the vehicle followed him.

Ling had made a U-turn and was now at the back of the vehicle that's following Rick Drago.

Making sure of the one tailing him, Drago made another turn, that's when Ling with his backup car closed in. Drago stopped the Range Rover at the side of a building and reverse as the vehicle tailing him couldn't escape with Ling and the other blocking from behind.

With guns in hand, Ling approaches from the right and his partner from the left. Drago got out of the Range Rover with his jacket open and the butt of Nellie in full view and walked to the vehicle.

Ling and his partner open the front doors of the car and ordered the men out, handcuff them, and put them to sit on the pavement as Drago watches the two sitting in the back seat.

As his partner keep watch on the men sitting on the pavement, Ling took one man from the back seat to his car, then Rick took the other one to his vehicle and sat him down.

The man reached into the inside jacket pocket. With a quick move, Nellie was in Rick Drago's hand and level at the man's heart.

"Just reaching for my ID," he said, in broken English.

"Why are you following me?" Rick asked.

"I'm following orders," the man said.

Ly Ling walked over to the Range Rover and talked to Rick.

"They are from the Ministry of Defense office and have orders to protect you."

"Protect me from what? why wasn't our Embassy informed me of this?" Rick Drago angrily asked.

"I don't know, I made a call to my superiors, they'll get back to me in a minute," Ling said.

Rick Drago let the man leave. He then called the Embassy and talk to Angel Cross.

"Cross. Who gave the order to have me followed?" he asked. "It nearly caused those men their lives."

"I know nothing about anyone following you. Who could be that stupid? They don't know who you are or what you do," Cross nervously said.

"Listen, Cross. If you're in bed with Futura, and if I get a glimpse of anyone in my rear-view mirror, you know how it will end," Rick said.

Rick didn't wait for an answer, he turns off the

phone, waved to Ling, got back into his vehicle and drove away.

Angel Cross, like many other office pencil pushers, had heard stories about an operative with many aliases, Rick being one of them, and here he was in Japan under diplomatic protection soon after the break-in at the Bermuda office.

Futura cell phone rings when he was about to leave his office.

"Hello, Cross, what's happening?" Futura asked when he answered the call.

"Rick knows," Cross said with a scary tone in his voice.

"What makes you say he knows?"

"It's what he said to me," Cross said. "He mentioned I'm in bed with you. It's a western saying when a person is doing something they shouldn't with another person, in this case it's our two countries."

"Then, fix the problem!" Futura exclaimed.

"I can't fix this, and you don't know who he is."

"Yes, I do," Futura replied.

"No, you don't. You only think you do. But you don't," Cross assured him.

"What are you trying to say? He's some special Diplomat," Futura shrugged.

"Yes, the kind no one fucks with," Cross yelled.

"Are you trying to scare me?" Futura asked nervously.

"No. I'm saying this to you. If you're thinking about making a move of this Diplomat, forget about it, that will end badly for you."

"We shall let him finish his stay and leave with no more incidents."

"Agreed," Cross said.

Chapter Twelve

One week later. London, England.

Rick stood on the second-floor deck of the sprawling house, gazing through the early morning London fog.

The woman standing next to him with her exquisite figure encased in a black cashmere sweater with a high neck is Kayla Grandison.

"This house has everything to offer four bedrooms, four baths, and a great view of its surroundings, Kayla said."Everything, except a man figure."

"Yes, it's beautiful and has a nice view," he said.

Kayla slipped her hand under Rick's arm and rested her head on his shoulder.

"What about the man figure?" Kayla questioned.

Rick put his arm around her shoulders and pulled her closer to him as he pondered the question asked by Kayla.

"It's tempting, but my work? I do a lot of traveling."

"So do I," Kayla responded.

Rick kissed her forehead, then passionately on her lips.

"I'm falling in love with you, Rick," Kayla continued. "And before you asked, I have no boyfriend, not dating anyone, have no kids, and was never married. I'm all yours if you want me. I know we didn't talk about this in Barbados, so I'm telling you now."

Rick has never thought about settling down and having a wife and kids.

After meeting Kayla in Barbados, the feelings Rick has for her, he had never felt for any other woman.

Rick has met many women from around the world in his travels; none of them has given him the feeling like Kayla has, a feeling of true love and respect.

Now here he was with Kayla, and she let her feelings for him known.

"I was hoping you would surprise me with a visit, and here you are," said Kayla. "I bought a few items for you."

"You shouldn't have done that," Rick suggested.

Kayla led him into the bedroom, opened one side of the vast clothes closet that took one entire side of the room, and showed him the items she had purchased.

Rick decided not to make any comments about the beautiful gesture Kayla had made by buying him gifts.

She then took him on a tour of the mansion, he had arrived late in the evening and didn't have the time to examine the estate Kayla call her home.

Oriental rugs in a variety of places throughout the home, with five bedrooms, each having a large screen TV, three of them with Jacuzzi, and walk-in closets.

The home also has cake shape chandeliers, a sturdy extendable dining table with matching chairs, an exercise room with the latest equipment, and a swimming pool.

As they walk outside, the gardener stopped trimming the hedges and wave at Kayla.

"Good morning,"Kayla continued. "He was working here when I bought this place, so I kept him on."

"That was nice of you," he replied.

"I also kept the housekeeper."

"Who looks after the pool when you're away?"

"If I will not be here for a long time, I always have the pool guy come over and shut it down until I return."

Kayla punched in numbers, and the door to the

garage opened.

"Here is my transportation," Kayla proudly said.

"Nice collection you have here," Rick assured her.

A 1940s Phantom Rolls Royce. 1994 Bently, a 1960 Triumph convertible and a 2000 Rolls Royce, all in showroom condition.

"Which one would you like to take out for a spin today?" Kayla asked.

"The one you haven't driven in a long time."

"That would be the 2000 Rolls," replied Kayla.

"Rolls it is," Rick stated.

The air was crisp. Kayla wore a grey fringe sweater tucked in at the neck with matching pants, and Rick dressed in a black hoodie and blue skinny fleece jogging pants. Something wet the grass beneath their feet when Kayla and Rick walked arm in arm around the grounds with the pruned grass and trimmed hedges, lush and lovely.

The Gazebo on the backside of the lawn big enough to accommodate four tables seating 16 people.

On one side was the place for refreshments fully stocked and on the other were where you can cook your meals outdoors.

Kayla and Rick enter the house after the walk around the grounds.

"What would you have for breakfast?" Kayla asked.

"I'm looking at it," he blurted out and winked when she looked at him..

"Okay, besides me, what would you like?"

"I'm not much of a breakfast person, a piece of toast, fruits, and coffee."

"Coming right up, darling."

"When are you leaving to go on your modeling assignments?" Rick asked.

"I'm leaving in four days and will be away for six weeks," said Kayla. " I have to do Brazil, Mexico, Korea, Japan, New York before returning for the London week."

"That's a hectic schedule," Rick said.

"It happens. Are you going to stay here until I return?" asked Kayla.

"No. I have to go to the office in New York, then back to Canada."

"Here's the security code for the house and a set of keys if you come back here before I return, you can let yourself in," said Kayla, handing the keys and code to Rick.

Rick took Kayla out for a night in London city, he made dinner reservations for two at the Aspers Casino.

Later that evening, he took the rolls out of the garage and parked it at the front of the mansion.

Before taking the Rolls Royce from the garage,

Rick hid a piece of his hardware in the trunk.

"Your chariot awaits," he said.

"Another minute or two, my dear," Kayla responded.

"No rush."

"Where are you taking me?"

"How about a little fun and games before you go off to work?" Rick queried.

"Sure," Kayla said with excitement in her voice.

"You sound like a happy camper."

"I guess I'm experiencing that feeling of a little girl opening her Xmas gift."

"Let's go!"

Rick eased the Rolls Royce out through the high wrought-iron gates of the mansion and sped away.

Sometime later, he stopped the rolls at the VIP parking area of the Aspers casino.

Giving the keys to the valet with Kayla on his arm, they walked to the dining room.

"What games do you play?" Kayla asked.

"I play poker, but tonight I'll try the roulette table."

"I've played nothing at the casino."

"Do you have a lucky number?" Rick asked.

"Yes."

"All you have to do is put money on the number at the roulette table!"

"Okay, then what?"

"If the ball stops on your number, you win."

"You'll tell me how much to wager?"

"How much you want to bet is up to you."

A few hours later, Rick and Kayla left the casino.

Rick broke even at the roulette table, while Kayla won 300 euros. Arriving back at the mansion, they took a shower together, went to bed, and made love in the early morning hours before falling asleep.

Thursday and Kayla are getting ready for her trip to Brazil.

"I'll drive you to the airport," Rick stated.

"I've notified the limousine service," Kayla replied.

"Call back and cancel!" he suggested standing in front of her, looking into her face.

"Okay darling," Kayla said leaning in and smacked a kiss on Rick's cheek.

"Today was Bently day," Rick said. "You should do the same things you always do when going away for a long time."

"But, you're here for another day, don't you need to have access to some items?"

"No, I'll be okay," he said.

"Will Michael be taking you to the airport tomorrow?" asked Kayla.

"He will."

The following day Michael picked Rick up at Kayla's mansion. He took him to the airport for the eight hrs American Airlines flight to New York.

"You look well-rested," Michael suggested. "Is it the London fog responsible for this, or something else?"

"I feel great," Rick responded with a smirk.

"From Barbados to London, this is serious, isn't it?" Michael asked with curiosity in his voice.

He smiled. "There's something about Kayla."

"Can I expect to be the best man sometime soon? You're not getting any younger, and maybe it's time to think about a family, mate."

"Never thought I'd be saying this, but you're correct, we're not getting any younger. And this business we're in, was meant for much younger people, not that we're over the hill," Rick said.

The two friends laughed.

"Speak for yourself!" Michael suggested bringing the car to a stop at the entrance to the airport.

Michael left the car and walked with Drago through the VIP boarding area and onto the plane.

"Goodbye, mate, the next time we meet. I hope to be your best man," said Michael, shaking Rick Drago's hand.

Rick thought about what his friend Michael had said about. Starting a family.

Kayla has never mentioned to him about marriage. She just said the mansion needs a man.

Rick knows if he settled down with Kayla, there would be many broken hearted women around the globe.

Eight hours later, he arrived in New York and checked into his suite at the Hilton Hotel.

The next morning Rick meet with Dan McCall at his office.

"Welcome back, Rick," said Dan McCall. "You look refreshed."

"And you look a lot older than I remember."

"I worry too much about Joanne," said McCall. "I know she can take care of herself, but I'll feel a lot better if you were close to her."

"Is there a problem?" Rick asked, sounding a little concern.

"No."

"Then stop your worries!" Rick suggested rather harshly.

"Now, we got names from the USB stick you took from the Japanese," said McCall, then a long pause.

"Okay, let me guess, his name is on it," Rick raised a brow.

"Yes, number two is Angel Cross," McCall replied.

"What are you going to do about it?"

"It's already taken care of, the day after you left Hong Kong we picked him up when he left home heading to his office."

"Where is he?" Rick queried.

"Here in the USA, we have him at the farm."

"Has he given us anything? "Rick inquired, somewhat disgusted.

"Yes. The technician there tried a new method, and the results proved to be rewarding."

"Did he say anything about the attack in Bermuda?" Rick asked, when the red phone on the desk rang.

"Yes," Dan said, putting the receiver to his ear for a few moments.

"I know that look," Rick continued. "Let's have it!"

"The Major General Ki Harada, and Arata Furuta were found dead this morning, shot execution-style sometime last night, while you were in transit coming here."

"Loose ends are being tied up," Rick suggested.

"I'll give this information to the technician at the farm to pass on to Angel Cross," Dan McCall said.

"What about Bermuda? Did Cross had

anything to do with what happened there?" Rick asked.

"They made him sweat for a few days before questioning him and then passed the other names on to Ly Wing in Japan. Any information gathers about the Bermuda affair. I'll pass it onto you."

"I will visit dad and spend some time with him," Rick said. "First, I have to go shopping and buy gifts."

"How is he doing?" Dan McCall, the section chief, asked.

"He's doing all right, he has the security firm keeping him busy," he replied.

"Why don't you take the jet, it's fuel and ready to go at a moment's notice!" suggested Dan.

"I'll take you up on your offer," Rick said.

"Good, I'll inform the pilot to expect you sometime later today," said Dan.

A few hours later, Rick finished his shopping and boarded the company jet for the five-hour flight to Arizona.

Waiting at the airstrip for Rick was Patrice Carlisle, his dad's private secretary.

"Hi there, handsome," said Patrice, excitement in her voice while she hugged Rick when he got off the plane.

"Hi, Patrice," Rick said with a smile. "Where is dad?"

"He thought you'd be glad to see me," Patrice said, while they walked from the plane and got into the car.

"My dad's still trying to make us a couple," Rick Drago said.

"I have no problem with that," Patrice said. "Some times, parents know what's best for their children."

Both of them laugh.

"You would say something like that," he said. "What about your boyfriend?"

"What, boyfriend? Who told you I have a boyfriend?" Patrice asked.

"You know how people talk, and I hear things," Rick said.

"I went out on a couple of dates with this fellow, nothing serious," explained Patrice.

"This fellow, does he have a name?" Rick said. " Is he someone I know?"

"His name's Gordon Jones," Patrice said. "You know him?"

"I don't think so; should I?" he queried.

"He knows who you are," said Patrice while she started the BMW and sped away from the airstrip.

Jennifer Ames was there to greet him when they arrived at the house.

"Welcome home, Mr. Rick," Jennifer said.

"It's good to be back."

Jennifer Ames was Thomas Williams housemaid and cook, although Rick believed she's more than a maid or a cook to his dad.

Thomas lives on a sixty-acre piece of land; he has a few cows and horses.

Seeing Rick and his dad standing together, anyone would think they were brothers instead of father and son.

Thomas employed one ranch hand to do chores around the property and tend to the animals.

Thomas Williams also owns a security firm with offices in Phoenix, Scottsdale, and Tucson, Arizona. He started the after retiring from the army where he held the rank of Sergeant Major in the Delta force division.

Thomas was born on the Island of Barbados, his parents Andrew and Paula Williams emigrated to the United States and settled in New Jersey when Thomas was five years old.

After graduating from college; Thomas Williams joined the military and had a distinguished career in the army.

During his time in the military, he met and married Marjorie Collins, a pilot in the United States air-force.

Richard David Thomas Williams, alias 'Rick,

is the product of that union.

Rick followed in his father's footsteps and became a member of Delta Force, earning the rank of lieutenant colonel before leaving the military.

Rick mother, Marjorie Collins Williams, lost her life when her fighter jet was shot down over Iraq during a fact-finding mission.

After meeting Jennifer. Rick then took his one piece of luggage and the gifts he bought upstairs to his room, then returns to the kitchen where Jennifer was preparing dinner.

"Something smells delicious," Rick said when he entered the kitchen.

"Special for you, Mr. Rick," Jennifer said.

"Why do you always call me, Mr. Rick?" he asked.

"Are you staying for dinner, Patrice?" asked Jennifer without giving him an answer to his question.

"Of course, I am staying," Patrice replied.

Patrice and Jennifer took the dishes into the kitchen.

Rick poured Cognac into three snifters and walked into the living room.

Moments later, Patrice and Jennifer enter the living room carrying chocolate cake, ice cream, and coffee.

"You're always trying to fatten me up every

time I return home," Rick said.

"Chocolate is good for you," Jennifer said. "The darker, the better."

"Yes, how often do you eat dessert, Rick?" queried Patrice. "And besides, you'll burn the few calories away quickly."

Jennifer looks at Patrice, and both of them smile.

"When is dad coming back?" Rick asked.

"Sometimes, he stays away for a few days depending on the situation," Patrice. explained

"Where did he go?" he queried.

"On this trip, he's in Scottsdale," said Patrice. "I have the number to contact him."

One hour later, Jennifer said goodnight and left the living room.

Patrice then sat on the sofa close to Rick.

"I'm staying with you tonight!" said Patrice.

"What about Gordon; won't he miss you?" Rick asked.

"I told you, it's nothing serious with Gordon and me," Patrice said.

They gazed at each other in silence until he raised his glass.

Patrice didn't raise her's. "I have something else to say, Rick. When I'm finished, we'll drink a toast and then make love, either here on the sofa, or in your room."

"You've decided to stay, then we'll go to my

room," Rick said.

"After much, much thought, I've concluded Rick, you're one of the world's prized bachelor," said Patrice before being interrupted.

"At least you've thought of me," Rick scowled.

"I also concluded about myself," Patrice continued. "I love you very much, and I will not have you for myself, so anytime I get to spend with you, I will make the most out of it."

Rick attempted to say something.

"Please don't interrupt!" Patrice exclaimed.

"I was about to say, let's go to my room." Rick said, while he raised his glass. Patrice picked up her own.

They touched the rims of the snifters, and Patrice took a swallow.

"There, the toast," she continued. "Now, I'm ready for you."

Rick got up from the sofa, took Patrice by the hand, and walked upstairs to his room.

"I'll freshen up," said Patrice, letting her clothes fall to her feet.

Looking at her magnificent body when she walked away from him, heading to the bathroom, Rick realized he's getting a hard on.

His erection grew massive when he laid on the bed, waiting for Patrice to return from the bathroom. He didn't have to wait any longer.

Patrice came strolling out of the bathroom

wearing only her birthday suit, seeing Rick penis upright, she engulfs it into her mouth, a few moments later, Patrice is riding it like a cowgirl. Patrice cried.

I love you Rick oh my God I love you so much increasing the frenzy.

Rick turned Patrice over on her back.

"Deeper, she cried, give it all to me: you magnificent animal."

Orgasm after orgasm burst out of Patrice; She clawed Rick back, pulling him down on her, harder and harder until their movements became synced.

The lovemaking wasn't violet, Patrice had left threadlike marks on his back with broken skin from her raking fingernails in a couple of places.

Patrice drew his face down to meet hers, then kissed him gently. He returns the kiss, his tongue moving over her face until their lips meet. Her tongue met his, and her hand found his dick.

"Rick, you're still hard," she whispered in his ear between kisses.

Rick didn't respond.

"Put it back in! Rick, let it sleep in me!" suggest Patrice, turning to lay on his left side with her back toward Rick.

They fell asleep; Rick awoke the next morning to find Patrice had left. On the nightstand was a handwritten note.

Rick read the note. "I had to leave early for the office, will call you later today, my love!" Patrice.

Rick looked at the clock on the wall in his bedroom; the time is nine-thirty am. He took a shower, dress, takes up the gift he bought for Jennifer, and went downstairs to the kitchen where Jennifer was making toast.

"You want something to eat?" she asked.

"No, I'll have a cup of coffee," replied Rick, taking the gift from behind his back and giving it to Jennifer. Then he opened the fridge and grabbed an apple.

Jennifer opened the gift. "Thank you, Mr. Rick."

"Thanks for what?"

"I thought you'd be famished this morning after your activities last night?' queried Jennifer.

"What activities are you talking about?" Rick asked.

"Sure, you don't need me to fix you something?" asked Jennifer continuing to toast two slices of bread.

Turning around from the toaster, she sees Rick staring at her.

"Rick, why are you looking at me like that?" Jennifer asked.

"What; oh, I've never seen you without your apron," he answered.

"Is that the real reason?" Jennifer asked.

"No, not really, I can see why my dad has you here at the house," stated Rick.

"Oh, care to tell me; I'd like to know," said Jennifer with a smile on her face.

"Now, remember, this is only my opinion," said Rick. "You have a beautiful face and a very appealing body."

"Appealing body? Never heard that one about my body before."

"That's my opinion."

"You like my body?"

"Who man won't," he shrugged.

"Enough about me and my body. What about you and Patrice?" asked Jennifer. "Are you two an item?"

"No, we make the best of each other company whenever we can. I meet someone on my last trip to Barbados."

"Care to tell me about her?" Jennifer queried.

"I will before I leave."

"Okay, I'll hold you to that."

"What would you like to do today now that my dad is not here?"

"I didn't think about it."

"It must be something you'd like to do, but don't because of your duty to dad."

Rick cell phone rang, he answered, it's Patrice on the line.

"You're up, sleepyhead. I had to leave early, and you didn't say how long you'd be staying," Patrice queried.

"I'm not sure, but it won't be soon."

"Good. You and I will have more time together," Patrice continued. "You know my heart belongs to only you, although I don't have yours ."

"We're going out, Jennifer and I."

"Okay, I will see you after I've finished work."

Rick went to the garage; minutes later, he returned with the Hummer. He parked and waited for Jennifer to join him.

Jennifer came out wearing white pants and a light blue color blouse, a straw hat on her head, a white scarf around her neck, a pair of dark sunglasses, and blue shoes on her feet looking more like the woman of the house instead of a maid.

The outfit fit her perfectly, especially her ass and showing the fullness of her breast.

"You're doing it again," she said, getting into the Hummer.

"Doing what?"

"Undressing me with your eyes," Jennifer said. "Let's go!"

RICK DRAGO WILL RETURN IN
BOOK THREE OF THIS SERIES.

"HELL IN PARADISE"

OTHER BOOKS BY
SHERWIN A. GOODMAN

SUSAN & FRIENDS

A SUMMER AT SEA. " SHORT STORY"

www.ingramcontent.com/pod-product-compliance
Lightning Source LLC
Chambersburg PA
CBHW070623130626
46556CB00001B/454